MW01231864

How to Raise
Your I.Q.
by Eating
Gifted Children

HOW TO RAISE YOUR I.Q. BY EATING GIFTED CHILDREN

Lewis Burke Frumkes

McGRAW-HILL BOOK COMPANY

New York   St. Louis   San Francisco   Bogotá
Guatemala   Hamburg   Lisbon   Madrid
Mexico   Montreal   Panama   Paris
San Juan   São Paulo   Tokyo   Toronto

Copyright © 1979, 1980, 1982 and 1983 by Lewis Burke Frumkes

All rights reserved. Printed in the United States of America.
Except as permitted under the Copyright Act of 1976, no part
of this publication may be reproduced or distributed in any form
or by any means, or stored in a data base or retrieval system,
without the prior written permission of the publisher.

First McGraw-Hill Paperback edition, 1984
 2 3 4 5 6 7 8 9 F G R F G R 8 7 6 5
ISBN 0-07-022102-2 {H.C.}
       0-07-022103-0 {PBK.}
Library of Congress Cataloging in Publication Data
Frumkes, Lewis Burke.
How to raise your I.Q. by eating gifted children.
I. Title. II. Title: How to raise your IQ by eating
gifted children.
PN6162.F76 1983   814'.54   83-7956
 ISBN 0–07–022102–2 (H.C.)
       0–07–022103–0 (pbk.)
Book design by *Judy Allan (The Designing Woman)*

for Alana

The following pieces were first published in *The New York Times:* "One Happiness Place" (under the title "The Inside Story on Co-ops"), "The Elevator—Some Highs and Lows," "Frumkes' Rules of Order," (under the title "A Motion to Second the Blurt"), and, in abbreviated form, "Letter to the 18th Floor," "Highlights of the Great International Film Festival and Cook Off," "Sending Parents Off to Camp," "Preparing Easter Eggs for the Holiday Season," and "Horoscopes." © 1977, 1978, 1980, 1982, 1983 by The New York Times Company. Reprinted by permission.

"Bay of Pigs, Take Two," "Willard's Words," "Notes from the Alumni," "Making the Inner Circle," and "A Guide to the Lesser Sheiks" first appeared in *Punch.* © 1977, 1978, 1981, 1982 by *Punch.* Reprinted by permission.

"A Volley of Words" first appeared in the December 1976 issue of *Harper's.* © 1976 by *Harper's Magazine.* Reprinted by permission.

The following pieces originally appeared in magazines in slightly different versions; "Urban Cowperson," "Exotic Gifts from Harry and Larry," and "The Case of Child C" in *The Mensa Bulletin.* "Class Joints in New York Nightlife," "Cull Deep Truths from Wedding Announcements," and "Chain, Chain, Chain of Fools" in *Louisville Today.* "Letters of Recommendation" in *The Graduate,* published by the 13-30 Corporation; "Tag-Sale Terror" in *Westchester Spotlight,* "Magic on my Mind" in *Genii,* "Gefilte Fish Pirates" in *National Jewish Monthly.* The remaining pieces are appearing for the first time.

Contents

ONE HAPPINESS PLACE   1

ELEVATORS AWAY   4

CLASS JOINTS   7

HOW TO RAISE YOUR I.Q. BY EATING   10
GIFTED CHILDREN

YOO HOO TAXI   14

URBAN COWPERSON   18

WEDDING ANNOUNCEMENTS   21

BIG DOINGS ON 18   25

GEFILTE PIRATES: SCOURGE OF SOUTH BAY   28

REAL ESTATE LISTINGS   31

MAKING THE INNER CIRCLE   36

NOTES FROM THE ALUMNI   40

CHAIN OF FOOLS   45

EXITUS   49

SHRINK STRIKE   54

A FRINKER BY ANY OTHER NAME   57

FRUMKES' RULES OF ORDER   61

APPLYING FOR THE JOB   66

LETTERS OF RECOMMENDATION   70

TOO BUSY GOING TO THE JOB TO MAKE ANY   76
REAL MONEY?

RUN, RUN, RUN   81

HIGHLIGHTS OF THE GREAT INTERNA-   84
TIONAL FILM FESTIVAL AND COOK-OFF

THE SOCIAL CLIME   88

AEROBIC TYPING   92

WILLARD'S WORDS   96

MET GIVEN $10 MILLION DRUG   100
COLLECTION

LOOKING FOR LA CREME DE LA CRUDE   104

RESEARCH INDICATES CARS MAY TALK   109

A GUIDE TO THE LESSER SHEIKS   113

COUP COUP IN THE SEYCHELLES   117

EXOTIC GIFTS FROM LARRY & HARRY   120

CUBA LIBRE	125
BUNNY BURGERMEISTER LOVES BOOKS	128
THE NEW PUNCTUATION	132
SENDING PARENTS OFF TO CAMP	136
PREPARING EASTER EGGS FOR THE HOLIDAY SEASON	140
TAG-SALE TERROR	144
A VOLLEY OF WORDS	148
MAGIC ON MY MIND	157
THE BOOK OF LISPS	161
CLOSE ENCOUNTERS OF THE FOURTH KIND	165
THE SUSHI OF LIFE	168
FUNDAMENTAL PRINCIPLES OF HYSTERIA	172
SPACE CHAT	175
THE SHAPE OF THINGS TO COME	180
THE CASE OF CHILD C	184
TV SPECIAL	189
AN OFFICIAL REGISTER OF IMPORTANT NAMES	193
HOROSCOPE	198

One
Happiness Place

*D*ear Tenant Stockholders:

During the past year we have made substantial progress toward our goal of utopian high-rise living at One Happiness Place.

Despite a deficit of $3.5 million for the fiscal year 1983, we anticipate no additional assessment to the tenants. This fortuitous state of affairs results primarily from the finance committee's successful marketing of our 8 percent Happiness Bonds of 1988, of which 90 percent were purchased by Mr. Rocco Corleone, Apt. 4B.

Concerning the security of the building, about which many of you were outspoken at the annual shareholders meeting, several measures have been implemented and others are under consideration to reduce the incidence of breached security in the building.

Mrs. Mandel, Apt. 12H, who chairs the security committee, reports that three of the four machine-gun nests ordered by the apartment corporation are now in position on the parapet walls adjacent to the penthouse. The fourth should be operational within the next six weeks.

In addition, the Happiness Vigilantes have been bolstered by four new troops, namely Mr. Cohen, Apt. 8E, Mrs. Velasquez, Apt. 9J, and the Rachmaninoff twins from 10D.

Mr. O'Hara, division commander, Apt. 2A, calls HV the finest regiment of its kind in the city and a model for security forces throughout the country. Only last week, HV all but decimated a mobile squad of enemy teenagers who had invaded our eastern flank on skateboards. No losses were reported, though Mrs. Negholt, 7J, suffered a sprained ankle in the skirmish. Mrs. Negholt has been replaced by Col. Hans Von Schmidlap, 3F.

Some of you have complained about the playing of "Hail to the Chief" which is automatically activated in the lobby whenever someone enters the front door. This matter was discussed at great length during our last meeting and it was suggested by our Treasurer, Ms. La Rue, that possibly "Hail to the Chief" could be replaced by "Night Train." By secret ballot, it was decided to retain "Hail to the Chief" through 1983.

Regarding gratuities to the staff, the board asks that the setting up of annuities and trust funds for favorite employees be discontinued. We realize that this innocuous little frivolity on the part of some of our older line members has become almost traditional, but for the benefit of our less affluent tenants, we ask that it be stopped. Another reason for curtailing this practice is the attrition of staff members, resulting from said practice.

As our year draws to a close, the board wishes to assure you that everything possible is being done to insure the continuance of that spirit of harmony and conspiration which has characterized One Happiness Place in the past. While 1983 has been a good year, we anticipate an even better one in 1984.

Your Board of Directors,
Coquelin de Panache, Pres.

Elevators Away

*T*he trouble with riding elevators is that there's hardly time to develop meaningful relationships, so what brief encounters occur tend to be uncomfortable and evanescent.

Of the riders themselves, most divide into two classes, the number watchers and the foot watchers, with the former being far the more numerous. The number watchers invariably enter the elevator and push the button for their floor destination, then fix their eyes on the lit numbers above the elevator door for the duration of the ride. This act apparently eases their anxiety and serves to notify other passengers that they do not wish to be disturbed.

The foot watchers are even more interesting. They too enter and push the appropriate floor button, but then they proceed to stare at their feet as if the feet would get off on the wrong floor if not carefully paid attention to. Actually, just last week a pair of feet did get off on the wrong floor at Saks Fifth Avenue and charged two dozen pair of basketball sneakers to its owner's account. Incidents such as this, though rare, are what convert number watchers to foot watchers.

Of course, there are always those who have not as yet declared for number or foot watching and left to their own devices must learn the hard way. Take for example the young man who finds himself alone on the elevator with an attractive member of the opposite sex, presumably female. He studies her with undisguised admiration for two or three floors gathering courage to make a move. Then, just as the propitious moment arrives and he introduces himself, "Hi, I'm Fred Hummentashen," the elevator opens and his quarry steps out, leaving the doors to close in his face. It is not really Fred's fault; he has chosen the wrong theater of operation and would do better back at the Ferris Wheel where he has been successful in the past.

Because the space is small, and the conditions often crowded, etiquette on an elevator is de rigueur. Thus it is considered poor form among regular riders to smell bad or shout "Fire!," nor is singing much smiled upon, especially the lesser arias from *Trovatore* and *Aïda*.

If you ride elevators with any frequency, as I do, you will soon become familiar with the names of certain elevator inspectors, whose dates of inspection appear on a white card posted just under the graphic description of the female genitalia on the front panel. I am always reassured to learn that "Clarence Pinko" inspected my elevator on September 18, 1932, and that probably any day now he will inspect it again. It is this knowledge that helps me deal with my long-standing fear of turbulence and getting stuck between floors. These fears are groundless, to be sure, and no more rational than the fear of turning into a carrot and being eaten by a large rabbit; still they exist and I am not alone in having them.

While the primary purpose of elevators is to get people where they are going, some of us prefer riding just for the fun of it. Here the different types of elevators become a consideration. Perhaps you want the rich appointments of an old cooperative elevator with mahogany paneling and an operator who offers a weather report even though you've just come in from outside. Or maybe it is the dank smell and stark surroundings of a large freight with its array of invert drawings and pithy aphorisms. For nostalgia buffs it may be the department-store elevators where you jockey for position in front of the elevator only to be trampled by two thousand stampeding shoppers, or the old hydraulic lifts which debark every Tuesday for weekend arrival.

Whatever your personal reasons, elevators tell you something about the world in which we live. They tell you that man is a vertical animal that likes to travel in herds; that lingerie can be found on the fourth floor to the right of electrical appliances; that for a total experience one need but call 933-1759, after eleven; that somewhere there exists a building composed of just the thirteenth floors missing from all the others.

Of the myriad elevators that abound, my particular favorites are the supersonic variety found in tall office buildings and skyscrapers. These computerized cubicles whisk you into the empyrean faster than you can say "Jack Robinson," if you still say that, and offer Muzak to make your trip as pleasant as possible. On a recent visit to one of the world's tallest buildings, I began to hear the "Ave Maria" as we soared past the ninety-fifth floor and a sudden calmness came over me. I knew then, I had finally found the true way.

Class Joints

*I*n the old days it used to fascinate me how certain restaurants and clubs could flourish by denying entry to
prospective patrons. It was infinitely simpler then to crash
the pearly gates of heaven than the iron gate of 21. St.
Peter somehow was always gentler in his dissuasion than
the praetorian guard of that latter establishment. Sher-
man Billingsley and Gene Cavallero for their part stood
service at the old Stork and Colony carefully sifting wheat
from chaff, and God himself I believe was turned back by
Angelo at El Morocco.

Of course, those were the good old days and standards
have changed since, away from blue blood and cobwebbed
money toward more democratic ideals. But what is true
is true. The verboten is always desired and the greater
the exclusivity it seems the greater the attraction.

Have you noticed how even today restaurants appear to measure themselves by the number of empty tables they can hold against the clamoring throngs outside? The most successful are the ones that declare themselves full when only the rear and side tables are seated.

"We can seat you either at 4 P.M. or at 4 A.M. two weeks from Tuesday," says the maître d'. "Shall I put you down?"

"Yes, a table for two, please, at the 4 P.M. sitting."

"The name?"

"Luckincup," I answer, wishing I could add Senator and Mrs., Count, or food critic for *The New York Times*, but I can't and the maître d' responds icily:

"Could you spell that please?"

4 P.M. arrives on time, a clear and optimistic Tuesday, and I march through the portals of Le Snoot eager to claim my prize.

The place is empty save for several score of busboys scurrying about like electrons in a crimson and crystal atom. Pierre, the maître d', greets me at the door with a puzzled look. "May I help you?"

"Yes, I'm Mr. Luckincup," I answer. "I have a dinner reservation for two at the four o'clock sitting."

"Oh yes, of course," says Pierre, scanning his reservation book. "Duardo, please take Mr. Luckincup to table fourteen."

Within moments I am seated at a small but sparkling table garnished with shining silver and a glass vase filled with fresh flowers. Unfortunately it is situated on the restaurant's exhaust vent; I can tell by the loud clattering and hoarse oaths emanating from within. I summon the captain to ask for a table change. He in turn summons Pierre and they confer hastily. Pierre approaches and politely asks what the matter can be.

"Kitchen," I mutter. "Too noisy, would like to change table please."

"I'm sorry, that's impossible, Mr. Luckincup; all the other tables are reserved."

I ponder this, noting the absence of any other diners in the house. "But—"

"I am sorry—there is nothing I can do," says Pierre and turns his back on me, signaling that the audience is over.

Smoke begins to rise from my head. It curls gently toward the ceiling and is sucked up by a duct. My reservation was made almost two weeks ago. I check my hands and my wife for signs of leprosy. There are none that I can detect; it must be something else.

Pride peering over my left shoulder urges me to leave. Reason over my right shoulder agrees. I get up from the table to leave. The threat goes unheeded as the captain sanctimoniously pulls the table away so as not to impede my exit. Passing through restaurant center I observe a man with leprosy being seated at a banquette. I quicken my pace and depart Le Snoot barking minor execrations under my breath. A drunk on the street thinks I am talking to him and gestures obscenely in my direction. As I return the compliment he enters Le Snoot. Twenty minutes later he has not reappeared and I dejectedly make my way to Burger King where I am warmly received.

The following evening I try my luck at Entre Nous and strike out. The place is half empty. At Pou Pou's it is the same story, and La Belle Epoque and Rimbaud. I am discouraged but not put off.

Next Friday I shall try the fabled Le Dupe; I understand they seat no one. It must be fabulous. How else could they turn everybody down and get away with it? Perhaps if I wear black tie . . .

How To Raise Your I.Q. by Eating Gifted Children

*S*cientists have long suspected a link between eating gifted children and raising the I.Q., but until recently no one has been able to prove it. Now scientists believe they have found evidence to support their theory. Two teams of researchers, one on a diet of gifted children, the other on a placebo, have turned in amazing results. The team eating only gifted children succeeded in raising their I.Q.s an average of fifteen points over a period of two years, while the placebo group remains as stupid as ever.

The implications are enormous. Not only may it be possible in the future to raise one's I.Q. by ingesting an occasional gifted child (there are approximately $2^1/_2$ million in the U.S. alone, 5 million drumsticks, etc.), but it may provide ecologists with a partial solution to runaway population.

Nevertheless, conservationists are up in arms. You can't have people running around just plucking children off the street, they say; not every child is gifted. It could turn into offspringacide.

Scientists are careful to point out that while studies have shown gifted children to be larger and more attractive in the main than ordinary children, not every large, attractive child is gifted. "Frequently a plump, juicy looking child is just well fed," says Dr. Heraldic Leap, director of Gifted Studies at Johns Hopkins University. He urges potential consumers to be sure the child they eat is indeed gifted if they expect to see any appreciable increase in their intelligence.

How can you be sure the child you eat is gifted?

Dr. Leap suggests acquiring your child from Mensa, the Bronx High School of Science, or any of the reputable rapid advance classes found in most major cities. Or, he says, obtain a certificate from the child's school verifying that he or she has scored in the top 2 percent on any standardized intelligence test. Most schools are very good about this and will go out of their way to provide documentation. Finally, he adds, "Gifted children just taste different."

The following recipes were supplied by the educational psychology department of Columbia Teachers College.

Gifted Child En Papillote (six servings)

En papillote means roughly baked in a bag. Thus you will need sufficient aluminum foil to wrap completely around your children.

3 moderately gifted chil-
dren, I.Q.s 130—140
broth or lightly salted bath
water
2 pounds butter
2 quarts of flour
$\frac{1}{2}$ gallon Coppertone lotion
1 gallon Tropical Blend oil
1 dozen eggs beaten

handful of cayenne pepper
handful of mace or nutmeg
handful of ground chives
bucket of finely chopped
mushrooms
salt and freshly ground
pepper to taste

1. Place the 3 gifted children in a small tub and add bath water barely to cover. Add hot water, reduce the heat, cover and simmer gently until the kids are pink enough to pinch, 25—40 minutes, depending on the size of your gifted children. Remove the children from the bath and cool. Carefully skin the kids with a court order.
2. Preheat solarium to hot.
3. Cut 3 pieces of aluminum foil large enough to make a body reflector for each child and spread the foil with half the butter.
4. In an enormous skillet or pan blend the other ingredients into a saucy lotion.
5. Place each child in the center of each square of foil and ladle some sauce-lotion over the top. Fold the edges of the foil and seal tightly by crimping the edges. Arrange on baking sheet and bake 10 minutes. Serve wrapped in the foil. Pale kids will require less cooking time.

Gifted Child Fricassee

Not for the squeamish. (See Cooking Gifted Children and Chickens, Terman-Perdue.)

Barbecued Gifted Child

$\frac{1}{2}$ dozen gifted children
flour

6 broom handles
Johnson and Johnson marinade

Lightly dust the gifted children in flour and douse with marinade. Attach each child to a broom handle and proceed to barbecue as you would an ordinary child.

Gifted Child with Rosemary

4 gifted children
1 handful salt
1 pound butter

4 children named Rosemary
1 dozen onions chopped
1 pint of vinegar

Allow children to play in the other ingredients overnight. Then pair each gifted child with a Rosemary, sauté lightly, and serve.

Yoo Hoo Taxi

*N*ew York, New York, wonderful town, that is until you have to get somewhere by taxi. Actually, I have long been a champion of taxis as a superior means of transportation, preferring them for their privacy to the subway or bus. In addition they offer the rider a unique opportunity to enlarge his fund of knowledge on any given subject, just ask the driver. Sometimes the driver will enlarge your fund whether you want him to or not.

New York taxi drivers seem also to possess a complete command of the idiom and with a little encouragement will display it at every turn. Routinely, some drivers will characterize a female motorist who cuts them off in graphic anatomical terms and then return to their ongoing sociological commentary as if nothing had happened. It is this endearing quality that causes so many civilized visitors from out of town to describe them as "colorful."

I have never quite understood why a taxi driver who cannot find your destination and who is surly to boot deserves a tip. In most other service businesses gratuities are granted on the basis of service above and beyond the call of duty. Not so with the taxi driver. He may drive as if he were the lead car on a Coney Island roller-coaster, verbally assault you with every indignity known to man, and still expect to be gifted with a tip. Brassy, if you ask me. Still I do tip, and kick myself each time when I fail to receive even a glance of appreciation. Of course, this attitude does not take account of those drivers who are friendly and courteous, who go out of their way to help old ladies and pick up pregnant women. These drivers deserve a tip; it's just that there are only three and they are on the endangered species list.

Despite the dearth of cabs when you want them, taxis can be amusing. They come in a variety of attractive colors, yellow, yellower, yellowest, and several different shapes. The shape I like best is the boxy shape of the Checker cab, which allows me to stretch my legs. Other shapes are "scrunch" and "mini-scrunch," the last of which resembles that little car in the circus that somehow accommodates seventeen Watusi clowns. But no matter which shape you choose you are still bound to the house rules of the drivers, usually emblazoned on bright little signs posted all over the cab. These rules permit no smoking, no eating or drinking, no breathing, and no making change for denominations larger than a quarter. Pay strict attention to these signs and you will receive a minimum of abuse. Disobey, and you will be treated to a volley of locutions seldom found in standard compendiums of English usage.

To make your ride as pleasant as possible the drivers

frequently go out of their way and hire celebrated interior designers to dress up the inside of their cabs. One sports a pair of sponge rubber dice, circa 1950, dangling from the mirror, while another features a panoramic series of family portraits on the front dash. Be careful, though, if the decor includes an overabundance of religious statuary—it may indicate that the driver is less than secure at the wheel.

Recently, there has been a phenomenon sweeping the industry that is rapidly becoming a new source of irritation. I refer to the pools of cars who band together for what are sanctimoniously called "radio calls." To wit, I am standing on the corner freezing my toes off only to be passed by four hundred taxis on radio call. It is infuriating. If they are not on radio call they are off-duty, an equally annoying state of affairs. Sometimes I am passed as well by vacant cabs, at which time I check my clothes to see what the problem is. A few weeks ago in order to avoid this dilemma I decided to play the game and try the radio call myself. It costs, I discovered, an ungodly three dollars over the meter and is unavailable when you need it.

For my test run I chose a stormy winter's evening when I did not wish to trust potluck standing on the corner. I dialed my special number and a voice answered by the name of "Hold." Before I knew it I was listening to a medley of musical selections featuring "Tank Wallace and his Merry Toons." Nevertheless I clung to the phone desperately for two or three weeks fearful that I would lose my only opportunity of securing a taxi. A voice finally came back to inform me that there were no cars in my area. The trick I discovered was to say right away you were willing to set up a trust fund for the driver.

Just the other day I called one of these numbers and immediately announced I was willing to pay through the nose. "How much?" said a voice on the other end. "What was the last bid?" said I.

Now don't get me wrong, I still like cabs when I can get them, and practically lust after them when I can't; but if this keeps up I am definitely going to buy my own cab.

Excuse me, there goes one now. Oh drat! It's a radio call.

Urban Cowperson

Whether you set out to rope your cockroach on foot or on horseback you will need a good, strong, thick line of cord for a lasso, preferably one made of twisted hemp or other strong fiber capable of holding the roach once you have lassoed him. Anything less is to risk his breaking the rope or chewing it through before you have him secured.

Roaches are tough. They are made out of iron which has been annealed through centuries of inbreeding and persecution. If you jump up and down on one you will break your shoe.

Orthopteran insects of the family Blattidae (one of the best and largest), roaches are characterized by a flattened body, rapid movements, and nocturnal habits. That last means they go to the cupboard for a late night snack around the same time you do, an ideal time to do your roping.

In order to have the best chance of surprising your roach, you should either camp out in the kitchen or come an hour earlier for your snack and hide behind the kettle. Assuming you have a horse, you may want to tether it to the refrigerator or the stove, in any event making sure it is well fed so it doesn't whinny. Stealth is crucial to your campaign.

Also, you will not want to ride sidesaddle during the roping sequence since roaches are very strong and could easily pull you off your horse and into the garbage pail or worse. A neighbor of mine riding sidesaddle recently was pulled off his horse and down the kitchen sink. Not even the maintenance men equipped with Drano and Liquid-Plumr could dislodge him from where he was stuck. Seasoned roachers ride Western with the rope firmly hitched to the saddle horn. This way they have a chance to dismount and trip up the roach while the horse holds him tightly in tow.

At this point let us turn our attention to the scenario as it probably will occur and how you the roacher will successfully deal with it.

Nine chances out of ten the roach will begin his approach to the kitchen near midnight, moving quietly along any of several predetermined routes. It might be a hallway, a wall, or a secret passage known only to him. You will hear him when he enters, however, because he will pause momentarily on the countertop and go "Heh, heh, heh!" just before attacking the food. Throw on the lights and mount your steed—it is now that the chase begins. Temporarily blinded by the light, the roach will run a broken-field pattern across the counter with you in hot pursuit. If he runs behind the toaster or orange-juice squeezer, favorite ploys, you must flush him out with shouts of "Wahooo, wahooo" until he is out in the open once again. As you chase him over the counter, sometimes up a wall, then on the counter, then on the wall, whirl your lasso in lazy loops above your head and continue to shout "Wahooo, wahooo." This will paralyze the roach with fear and he will stop dead in his tracks. Precisely at this moment you must let fly your lariat, dropping it smartly around his belly and pulling taut. As he falls to the ground stunned, leap from your horse and turn the roach on his back, making sure to lift his forelegs first. This may not prove easy, of course, since the roach will be bucking and kicking his six legs in all directions. Once on his back, though, he is relatively harmless and you may proceed to brand him with your initials or corporate logo.

The branding done, your work is over. Why not cut the roach loose, open the refrigerator, and pour yourself a cold glass of beer? You deserve it.

Wedding Announcements

*T*he society page, especially that part that deals with wedding and engagement announcements, is more than just a way to save printing and postage costs in telling of a son's or daughter's betrothal; it is a clarion declaration of one's bloodlines and accomplishments.

Now to some of you bloodlines may not seem important, either because you do not have any, or because they run thin in spots; but to the rich of cell they are even more important than the considerable fortunes passed on to them by their wise and farsighted ancestors.

Indeed, while bloodlines may come first, accomplishments such as the inheritance of a New York Stock Exchange company or acceptance into a secret society are also steely marks of worth not to be ignored. Large looms the small-town plumber who is also a member of Skull and Bones.

Personally I find reading the society announcements every bit as fascinating as the Egyptian Book of the Dead, the special crypto-words and names telling me not only a family's history, but its current rank and standing; whether it has depth in greenbacks or just blue erythrocytes.

There is no easy Rosetta stone for deciphering these, but practice will increase your facility. Start with the following blurbs culled from my local paper and see how you do.

FRICK—POPOVER

Mr. and Mrs. Van Wyck Frick have announced the engagement of their daughter Doo Doo to Mr. C. Livingston Popover, who manages his own trust.

Doo Doo, who is known to her friends as Puff Puff, or to her very close friends as Dee Dee, or to the senior class at Dartmouth as Eee Zee, attended Miss Pinball's School in South Braintree where she was voted most likely to become pregnant during inclement weather.

Her grandfather, Col. Summerfield Frick, invented the cummerbund and was chairman of the Frick Formalwear Corp., which dispensed free cummerbunds to our troops during the Vietnam war. Her father, Van Wyck Frick, runs a polo league for advantaged children in Palm Beach.

Mr. Popover is the son of "Pop" Popover, the World War II ace who was twice decorated by President Truman and later sent to Leavenworth penitentiary for shooting down four civilian aircraft en route to Miami Beach. His mother is the former Abigail Oaktop, whose family has large holdings in real estate, banking, and the United States government. The couple plan a June wedding.

ALLISON PEAWORTH
ENGAGED TO NOBODY

Allison Peaworth, daughter of Admiral and "Money-bags" Turner Peaworth, has become affianced to Jeffery Sider, a nobody.

Miss Peaworth, who attended Hollyville Academy, Le Nevrose in Geneva, and Bennington College where she was graduated magna cum laude in creative movement, is working at the Morgan Guaranty Trust bank in New York as a blank check. Her maternal grandfather, Hoghorn Pill, discovered money.

The couple plan to be married in June and honeymoon aboard the family yacht U.S.S. *Lexington*.

C. W. CORLEONE
WEDS FIFI DUBOIS

In the Wood Presbyterian Church yesterday afternoon, Fifi Aubusson Dubois, daughter of Mr. and Mrs. Brian Dubois of New York and Block Island, was married to Carmine (The Wrench) Corleone, son of Don and Mrs. Rocco Corleone of West New York, certain parts of Detroit, and Las Vegas, Nevada. The ceremony was performed by Rev. Castiglia Maione, an employee of the bridegroom's family. Miss Camilia Dubois, sister of the bride, was maid of honor. For the groom, Angelo (The

Sub) Argutti served as best man in place of Bongo (The Nerve) Tuttifiore, who was detained when his head got unexpectedly lodged in the tail pipe of a Boeing 747 bound for Okinawa.

The bride was presented at a dinner given by her parents in 1971 and was a member of the Junior League, the Junior Assemblies, and "Bunions For Bertha," a militant podiatric group out of South Orange. She attended the Tingly Country Day School and was graduated from Le Snoot College in Marseilles, France. Her father is retired board chairman of Fenton, Hargewick, McDiggle, and Dubois, makers of "Groverly." The bride's maternal grandfather, Auchindrake Foxglove, was master of the hounds at Le Club.

Mr. Corleone is an alumnus of the "Cavoon" school in Castellamare, Sicily, where he was a member of "Wire and Shiv" and editor of *On The Take*. His father, who recently acquired Chicago as part payment of an outstanding debt, is a presser at the C & D laundry in lower Manhattan.

After a brief honeymoon the couple will go into hiding.

Big Doings on 18

*I*t hardly seems possible that I have been entertainment
director of the eighteenth floor for almost twelve years
now, but I have, and I love it. In fact, I was reelected this
year by the largest plurality ever, a unanimous vote actually, and a feat equal to any in our building's history.

True, Mr. Rodriquez on the fourteenth floor has held
the post longer, twenty-seven years if I remember correctly; but then the fourteenth floor is a dictatorship and
cannot in all fairness be compared with a floor like the
eighteenth, which elects its officers and treasures its for-
ward-looking constitution and hall lighting fixtures.
Rodriquez has to be constantly vigilant and watch his
flanks lest insurgents like the Young Turks from the
eighth floor invade his territory and remove him from
power. Only last week an attempt at removal was made.
Fortunately, one of his loyal lieutenants, a Mrs. Grady

by name, found him squooshed into a garbage-disposal bag bound for the basement and extracted him before any permanent damage could be done. But for her quick thinking and mouth-to-mouth resuscitation, the four-teenth floor would now be annexed to the eighth. In re-taliation Rodriquez sent a nocturnal team of two large dogs and a loose parrot to soil the eighth-floor carpets. The war goes on.

But enough of intrabuilding friction and skirmishes about which you could probably care less, or petty gossip relating to our tenants whose comings and goings are attended by flashbulbs; they are considered reporter-bait. You are rightly interested in how I entertain the eight-eenth floor and what new events I have scheduled for the coming year.

Consider first of all that the range of entertainment that I introduce on eighteen must be consonant with the overall philosophy of 901 East 83rd Street, a.k.a. "The Preakness," which states that the activities conducted here must always be of a nature refined; luxurious, but never loud. There are exceptions, of course, such as the blast for 2,500 thrown last February by the young Saudi couple in the penthouse, who hired a Marine Corps marching band, two rock groups, and 150 skimpily clad odalisques and exotic dancers as preprandial diversion for their guests before the fireworks display being launched from the roof got under way. But for what it's worth, we have not had a fuel shortage since, nor do we expect one until the year 2680, and then only if the young Saudi couple decides to move out. Personally, I don't think they will, since our building has all the luxuries and amenities of the desert without the sandstorms and ubiq-uitous camels. Camels, despite what most people think, represent a terrible source of annoyance to high-born Saudis like the El Figs, who for some ungodly reason associate them with bad luck.

But what are my near-term plans for eighteen? Tomorrow morning after the vacuum races at nine, there will be a morning tea hosted by Mrs. Winchell in 18C. Mrs. Beckerman, 18G, will provide the gin and Mrs. O'Hare, 18M, will clean up. Friday morning, Mrs. O'Hare will provide the gin and Mrs. Beckerman will clean up.

Saturday is the big day when all the eighteenth-floor children under five will be auctioned off to the other tenants in the building in an effort to reduce the noise level on eighteen. Mothers with children in the auction have been busy throughout the week powdering and oiling. If all goes well, Sunday will be spent alternately listening to the quiet and applauding.

In the unlikely event that it rains inside Mr. Garfoil's living room on Saturday and the auction has to be canceled, I have arranged for home movies to be shown in 18F, the home of Mr. and Mrs. Floyd Larkwind. Featured after the cartoons are the children of Mr. and Mrs. Larkwind swimming in Florida at various stages of their development. There is also some curious footage of Mr. Larkwind's mother knitting herself into a cocoon.

Monday the fourteenth, there will be an early-bird croquet match in the elevator hall beginning promptly at 5:30 A.M. and ending when one team or the other has had it. Apartments 18Q and 18A have volunteered to be goals. After the men have gone off to work there will be an all-day exchange of tidbits and news in Mrs. Gossamer's apartment, 18L.

At the moment I am not looking beyond next Monday, though I am aware that the eighteenth-floor Olympiad looms ahead, and also the "Buzzer" party, Odds and Evens, and the "Spouse Catch."

Why am I not looking further ahead? May I be frank? The seventeenth floor has made me a six-figure offer. How can I refuse?

Gefilte Pirates:
Scourge of
South Bay

*I*t's gefilte fish season, and the pirates are out in force again in the Great South Bay.

According to Sven Goldstein, one of two hundred baymen who make a living by shell fishing, the pirates began hauling away the best of the catch as soon as word got out that the gefiltes were in.

The pirates are baymen who take more than the legal limit of fifty jars a day, or who stay out after sundown, or who use forbidden bait such as "traife" to catch the fish. By some estimates pirates account for more than 75 percent of the boats working the cold waters in the Great South Bay. Such pirating is punishable by fines of from $250 to $1,000 for a first offense, death for a second offense, and confiscation of the boat and equipment in the event of a third offense.

The gefilte beds have been depleted over the years by overharvesting and periodic scarcities of the jellied consommé in which the gefiltes spawn. However, the 1982 supply of gefiltes for both the pirates and the legitimate baymen grew well despite these adverse conditions. Scientists from Zabar's and other leading marine research centers are studying the 1982 harvest in the hope of learning just why it survived.

One theorist speculates that it may have been due to the absence in the bay this year of the "gefilteblast," a natural predator that snatches up young gefiltes and uses them to caulk windows.

Emerson Nosepullet of the National Fisheries Service says that the baymen brought in 290,268 pounds of gefilte fish worth $5 million during the 1982 season. Most of the harvest, he says, went to a surprise new market— Japanese restaurants, who have been selling the gefilte as "koshermaki."

Mr. Goldstein pointed to two boats flying the dread skull and crossbones from their jibs. "There they are," he cried, "gefilte pirates right out in the broad daylight. What chutzpah! Honest fishermen like us don't have a chance."

The lead boat, *Nosh II,* suddenly dove from sight; it was a submarine equipped with a large shovel for a nose. Goldstein began to taunt the pirates with four-letter words, which he learned during a stint in the Navy, and had to be restrained.

Under state law, the baymen are not supposed to harvest more than their fifty jars of gefilte fish a day; and on boats with crews of more than one person, the limit is one hundred jars per day. The law was enacted in the late sixties to prevent overharvesting. But the pirates do not observe these limits and apparently split their hauls into fifty-jar lots so their buyers will not catch on.

Hauling gefilte fish is hard work. The baymen use steel

dredges and horseradish to trap the gefiltes as they roll along the bottom of the bay in their never-ending search for parsley and carrots. Then they empty the dredges into the boat and separate the round gefiltes from the potato-shapes. "Roundies," as the little spheres are called, are much cherished on the Upper West Side of Manhattan and Queens, but the potato-shapes are preferred among real cognoscenti. These days with fewer and fewer baymen working, and the pirates wreaking havoc among the beds, gefilte fish is fast becoming as sought-after as white truffles and Iranian caviar. What makes a good gefilte fisherman?

"It's mostly stamina," says Mr. Goldstein. "It takes a long time to get good. You have to develop a feel for when the gefiltes are rolling."

It is also a frustrating business. On a recent day, for example, Mr. Goldstein harvested less than one jar of gefilte during an entire hour of fishing. The wooden arm on his dredging tool had snapped and a replacement would cost thirty-five dollars, he said.

Meanwhile the pirates in their submarines were running amok at the bottom of the bay.

Real Estate Listings

*T*he housing market these days seems to have become so tight that prospective buyers are willing to give anything just to find a roof over their heads. Sympathetic real estate agents, cognizant of the desperate situation, are turning up new and unusual forms of habitation in a humane effort to satisfy their clients. These from the listings of Last Resort, Inc.

ANIMAL LOVERS (N.Y.)

By sheer good fortune one of the limited number of cages at the Central Park Zoo has come available. This particular cage, formerly occupied by Stuffy, the spider monkey, who is on loan to NASA for an indefinite period of time, fronts directly on the seal pond. It is equipped with parallel bars, hanging rope, and built-in concrete water trough. Unlike many cages at the zoo, Stuffy's has a private alcove ideal for those who are shy about dressing or sleeping in front of crowds. This sensational value is only $1,200 per month. Grapes included.

PLUTO'S RETREAT (N.Y.)

Deep below the hubbub and frazzle of the city, in a subterranean cavern abutting the Seventh Avenue IRT, lies this fabulous secluded three-room getaway. Once the summer residence of Carmine "The Eggplant" Tetrazzini, former capo di tutti capi of the Mafia, it has been used to entertain heads of state, famous entertainers, and members of the L and T Laundry.

Only yards from municipal transportation, this special bulletproof apartment is a must for anyone seeking to escape from it all. $3,000 per month includes two security guards and a year's supply of subway tokens.

APARTMENT IN THE SKY

The Space Agency has announced that it will lease one of its orbital laboratories as an apartment for a period of three years or until reentry, whichever comes first. This commodious nose cone, capable of accommodating two persons comfortably and a small disposable animal, is fully equipped with the latest equipment for viewing the moon, the planets, and the U.S.S.R. It has two berths, a head, and an eight-track tape system programmed to play "One small step for man; one great leap for mankind" over and over again at the push of a button. This magnificent opportunity to see the world from your apartment every hour on the hour is offered at just $200,000 per month.

ESTATE SALE (Virginia)

Set on one-quarter acre in the fabled "Sleepy Hollow" section of Arlington National Cemetery, this magnificent turn-of-the-century mausoleum has recently been converted into a jewel-like cottage with fireplace by the executors of the estate. Constructed entirely of Carrara marble with rose window and copper sleeping accommodations for twelve (six above ground, six below), this rustic little fortress is a perfect home for lovers of peace and tranquillity.

Price of $350,000 includes perpetual care and name change.

OCEAN VIEW (California)

Live like Jacques Cousteau in this quaint iron bathyscaphe anchored off a jetty in Marina Del Mar, California. $500 per month entitles you to unhurried views of exotic flora and fauna, pressurized cabin, and the right to be surfaced once a month. Photograph intrepid bathers right from your living-room window, or sharks, or both. *A real energy saver for ecology buffs.*

DIAMOND IN THE ROUGH

An entire five-story building in the South Bronx is available for just $36. Interesting weatherbeaten exterior gives way to minimum-look interior with scorched natural plumbing. Ideal for architect or construction engineer with firm grip on reality. *Needs work.*

ARBOREAL DREAM

Overlooking twenty manicured acres of industrial clover this, no expense spared, tree house on the property of Mr. and Mrs. H. Cullen Smith of Great Barrington, Massachusetts, is an outdoorsman's paradise. Built for the Smiths' children who are now in California finding their own space, this 10′ × 10′ oak and plastic lodging offers a complete kitchen by Coleman, furnishings by Eddie Bauer, and a crimson and black silk parachute for rapid egress. A steal at $800 per month, this lofty home won't last long.

SOLID INVESTMENT

Located 200 feet underground, this empty silo, once the home of a Minuteman ICBM that was launched last

Fourth of July after a party at the national command base in Omaha, can be yours for the asking.

While stark in appearance, silos are much in demand by security-conscious military buffs, and tall people who wish privacy. This particular silo is guaranteed to withstand even a direct hit by an enemy missile. Price on request.

Making the Inner Circle

*T*his year I have qualified for God's Inner Circle. True, I am not one of God's "Pals," which would have required a contribution of $100,000–$1,000,000, or one of God's "Chum's," $50,000–$99,999, or even one of God's "Friends," $25,000–$49,999, plus two good deeds. But I did make God's "Acquaintances" for $10,000, six good deeds, and a strong recommendation from Pastor Mc-Quee. I was very lucky. Harold Schnibble gave $10,000, managed two good deeds, and still didn't make it. Fortune smiled on me, and Pastor McQuee loves his pseudo-vicuña coat. An Acquaintance of God is still part of God's Inner Circle and is guaranteed a place on the waiting list for heaven when he dies. Pastor McQuee and the church board assured me that for another $5,000 I could reserve a place on the waiting list for my wife too, but I need time to think on that one. My kids tell me that for $5,000 and our old car, Harry, I could probably get that new station wagon they've been wanting. I know we could paint the other half of the house for $5,000. And more than likely $5,000 would cover the new overcoat, tweed suit, two pairs of slacks, three sweaters, and four shirts I purchased at Paul Stuart last week. (If one is going to be God's Acquaintance one has to dress like God's Acquaintance.)

Being a member of the Inner Circle also has definite advantages. For example, my pew, number 47, also known as the "Algonquin," now falls within the first fifty at church services and is carved. The carving on the "Algonquin" is of a pine tree rampant, beneath which lies a small bunny in the rigor-mortis position. Two hunters with a smoking elephant gun look on. An elephant smiles behind a bush. It means nods of acknowledgment, as if to say "How are you?" from other members of the Inner Circle and glares of envy from numbers 51 to 400. I love that part. It means that I no longer have to wave frantically to get the pastor's eye and that he knows who I am. "Vicuña coat, vicuña coat." It means that the pastor has me on his list for house calls—that he will visit our home once a month for tea and gossip. He will let us know which couples have split and who is a pervert. This month Roger Whippersnapperspoon is a pervert, which we knew anyway.

Perhaps I haven't properly conveyed what it means to be an Acquaintance of God, to walk into church of a Sunday morning or at Eventide and sit in pew number 47, the "Algonquin," which is situated between the "Mandrake" and the "Toledo." It is exhilarating and uplifting. It is also but a stone's throw to the Chums and Pals who occupy the roped-off section up front with the canopy and pews carved by Thomas Chippendale himself. The pews are condos, each owned outright by numbers 1 to 14, the Chums and Pals. And I sit not very far away. Uplifting did I say? It is positively mind-blowing.

The Inner Circle is a charmed circle, a magic circle, but then what would you expect for ten grand? Who can forget the time Paul De Winter of the Winterhaven De Winters, number 74, pretended to be lost and planted himself squarely in "Toledo" center? A bolt of lightning, a roll of thunder, and, whammo! Paul found himself high in the belfry serving time as a clapper. Paul has repented since, and moved up slowly from 74 to 63; but his head still looks like a flatiron, and if you hold him gently to your ear like a seashell and listen carefully, you may still hear him ring.

As an Acquaintance of God I am entitled not only to a place on the afterlife waiting list for heaven, and a carved and titled pew, but also, as I have mentioned, to a visit from the pastor monthly. Chums invariably make heaven nine out of ten times whether they have sinned or not, receive visits from the pastor weekly, and occupy the choice condos left of pulpit. Pals become intimates of God immediately after they die, or, if they give enough, sometimes before they die, and get to know God "up front and personal."

This year I have been asked to serve on the executive recruiting committee of our church as a hook. The executive committee's job is to increase membership in God's Inner Circle from 50 last year to 120. To do this we have made a deal with God to forgive up to 10 percent of a member's sins, not including food sins. Food sins, as you know, are unforgivable. God has agreed to this arrangement and there will be a phonathon sometime within the next two weeks. As for the potentially big givers, the so-called "fat cats," God has taken it upon himself to call them direct—no phone—either by burning bush or vision. "Hi! John, over here in the flames."

For my part, I have already begun recruiting—to hell with the phonathon. Wouldn't you really like to join God's Inner Circle? Tell the truth. Pew number 38, the "Brevoort," a real beauty, is coming available. Sign up now, and for one week only, you heard me, one week only, God will grant any prayer . . . Even food!

Notes from the Alumni

1902

From Pasadena comes word that Katrina Bushy Laidlow has had her name legally changed to Non Compos Mentis at the suggestion of her only daughter, Arrugula, who felt it was more in keeping with her present station in life. Mrs. Mentis also reports that she sneezed twice in March, wreaking havoc among the articles on her tea tray.

1915

On October 31, Mr. and Mrs. Frank "Limpy" McGillicutty celebrated their sixtieth wedding anniversary by going door to door on a fund-raising campaign for your alma mater. To date the school has received four Snickers bars, sixty-eight pieces of unwrapped chicken corn, three apples (only one of which was laced with rat poison), twenty-two assorted packages of gum, and a Snoopy wrist watch as a result of their efforts. Limpy adds that it was "Tanko" Harris, '17, who gave the Snoopy watch, grudgingly.

1921

A collection of light verse by Abdul Mohammed Kawaski Dada, who some of you may remember as Paul Cohen, has been published by the Revolutionary Press of Santa Ana, California. It is entitled *Primer on Subversive Techniques to Be Employed in the Violent Overthrow of Fascist Capitalist Governments, or In Your Face, Sucker,* and may be mail-ordered from either the publisher or *Paul's agent, Mohammed Light Year, while Paul is away on vacation for ten years to life.*

1938

Irving Beerstein has turned into a Collie.

1944

Randy Marauder performed his first coronary bypass operation last month in Montgomery, Alabama. This was too bad for the patient as Randy is an accountant.

The Monroe sisters, Janet and Gloria, who have been sitting in eggcups in their hometown of Spoonbill since last January, report that eggcup sitting is starting to catch on.

1950

The Harold Orthornes have moved from northern California to southern California where Harold is a roadblock for the Motor Vehicle Bureau.

1955

Rapunzel Headbinder Doolittle is now shooting up Valium full-time and reports that "all God's children have legs."

"Clubber" Mongialati was recently promoted to assistant consigliere in the Garbacho Mafia family. Any of you who need someone rubbed out, or just good advice, write "Clubber."

Taki Takahashi has opened his own Japanese restaurant in New Orleans where he is affectionately known as "Old Tempura Nose."

1959

Puffer Adams, after taking an advanced degree in physics, has created Milk of Magnesia Plus for the Phillips Company.

1960

After fifteen years in the swamps of Florida and Louisiana, Rowland Durkmeyer has now settled in Sarasota where he is a partner in Gribbet & Co., makers of "Yoo Hoo" frog calls.

"Dwarfy" Haynes is a psychiatrist in New York specializing in short people.

From Bethesda comes word that Michael Broadwind has received a grant from the federal government to study the long-term effects of lynchings on victims. Prior to receiving the grant Michael was a "good old boy."

Hemphill Mustardplaster III has been hired as a blank check by the Morgan Guaranty Trust.

Milly Hatbox is in the litigation department of Frawley, Mudbaum, and Mink, 50 Broad Street, and doesn't know how to get out. If someone would be good enough to notify a friend or close relative, they may pick her up any weekday between nine and five.

Chester Kravitz has written a definitive book on parking violations entitled *Back in with Impunity,* to be published by Viking in the fall. The book has already been selected by the AMA as an emetic.

Some other career changes have been received:

Ossie Origno is a fullback with Aetna Life in Hartford. Previously he was a fullback with Prudential.

Mary Jo Pullmancar is working as an electrode at the Stop'n Save sperm bank in Cedar Rapids.

1979

Cissy Sterling Moody gave birth to a daughter, Mary Silverplate Moody, on July 11.

Chain of Fools

*E*very now and then since I was twelve, I have had the good fortune to receive a chain letter in the mail and pass it on to my ten dearest friends. After all, when one is about to come into ten thousand golf balls, there is no reason to be selfish.

If not a golf ball, these letters invariably ask me to send out some other personal item, such as a five-dollar bill as a token of good faith. Within a short time, they promise, I will become richer than Saudi Arabia. At last count I have not become richer than Saudi Arabia, nor have I been turned into a small Buick as one particularly menacing letter said I would if I broke the chain.

All things considered, chain letters are a unique experience, and so I pass this one on to you.

Dear Pilgrim,

This is a chain letter. It was begun in 1794 in Lourdes, France, and is still circulating today in 916 countries around the world, including Great Britain. The original letter was written by a monk or monkey (the writing is not clear) who was down on his luck. He sent out one hundred copies of this letter and within two years received his very own parish or one hundred thousand bananas (again the writing is not clear). Suffice it to say that in the 185 years since the inception of this letter, millions of people have received good luck in one form or another.

In 1924 Mrs. O. R. Joglin of South Wales, Indiana, who was suffering from terminal cancer and given only two weeks to live, received this chain letter in the mail. She promptly sent out ten copies of the letter to her friends and on her way home from the post office stumbled across a gold mine.

But Mrs. Joglin was not the only one to have received good luck. Legion are the cases of people winning *Reader's Digest* lotteries or Jungle Gardenia perfume by Tuvache, or being elected president of their co-op. Their number is endless.

However, if you fail to carry out the message and spirit of this letter and break the chain, bad luck is sure to befall you. You may be butchered by an electric buzz saw, eaten by a manticore, or discover you are unable to find competent help. I certainly wouldn't want to be in your shoes with a doppelganger following me.

Not long ago Mr. McCuen Weebank of East Islip, Long Island, went to visit relatives in Harrisburg, Pennsylvania, after having broken the chain and received a lethal dose of radiation from the Three Mile

Island nuclear plant. On the way back to East Islip, his nose fell off. Shortly thereafter the entire McCuen family was ground into hamburger in an unusual highway accident involving their Toyota station wagon and a Boeing 747.

Check around with your friends, especially the ones who have just been divorced, lost their jobs, or smell like liver. Chances are they broke the chain.

Remember, Pilgrim, all you have to do to receive the Luck of the Monk is to make one hundred copies of this letter, adding your name to the top of the list and crossing out the name at the bottom. Then send them to your best friends and relatives. Within a month you will join Mrs. O. R. Joglin and the millions of others since 1794 who understood the power of the chain. The choice is yours.

Lewis Burke Frumkes
New York, N.Y.

A. Percival Cagutz
110 Weevil St.
West Boatswain,
    Oklahoma

Dr. Richard Frances
200 Moolus Strip
Philadelphia,
    Pennsylvania

Nicholas Golden II
Box 425
Butte, Montana

Dorothy Pittman
Minustown, Maine

Brigadier General David
    "Eyes" Pearce
PO Box 57
Hen's Teeth, North Dakota

E. Michael Stein
20–47 Green St.
Brownville, Maryland

Josephina Hernandez
4 Gracie Balcony
New York, New York

Richard von Zorn
29 Clover Patch
South Wales, Indiana

John Huegel
110 East Drimmer
Dan O River, Kentucky

Exitus

EDEN: ADAM, FIRST MAN, DIES

Adam, or "Man" as he was known to friends, died Monday night, apparently from the effects of a snakebite which he had suffered the previous day in his garden. His age at death was undetermined.

Adam spent the better part of his life in the pursuit of the knowledge of good and evil, which he eventually acquired. (It is good to love your brother. It is evil to put your brother's head in a vice and squeeze it until he apologizes for all the nasty things he has said to you, even though he probably deserves it.)

Adam is probably best remembered as having been the

first man. Besides his widow, Eve, he is survived by two sons, Cain and Abel.

NOAH: BOAT BUILDER DROWNS

Noah, who saved both man and beast from the Great Flood, drowned last Friday after having slipped in his bathtub. A boatwright by profession, Noah spent nine months aboard his great ark, *Hilda II,* with seven pairs of every clean creature after the catastrophic forty-day and forty-night deluge.

He is credited with having extracted a promise from you know who to never again destroy the world in a fit of rage. Noah negotiated a rainbow as the sign of that promise.

He is survived by his wife and three sons, Shem, Ham, and Japeth.

ABRAHAM, FATHER OF ISRAEL, SUCCUMBS TO OLD AGE

Abraham, ne Abram, who, for much of his life lobbied with the heavenly powers on behalf of his people, died yesterday at a very advanced age.

With Lot, Abraham co-founded Israel, which was originally called Canaan (not New Canaan, just Canaan). Late in life Abraham's wife, Sarah, was blessed with a son, Isaac, whom Abraham, during a particularly severe religious fit, almost did away with. In subsequent years Lot left Israel to work for Sodom, which never quite caught on. Abraham continued alone and Israel prospered under his aegis.

He leaves a wife, Sarah, and an only son, Isaac.

Funeral services will be held at Temple Beth Israel tomorrow at noon.

In lieu of flowers, the family requests that a lamb or first-born son be sacrificed.

EGYPT: JOSEPH, PHARAOH'S ECONOMIC ADVISOR, DEAD

Joseph, who for many years was chief economic advisor to the Pharaoh, died in his sleep last night.

Joseph, one of twelve brothers, left home at an early age to work in Egypt. He had the uncanny ability to predict agricultural trends and made a small fortune in the futures markets before seeking service with the Pharaoh.

His book, *Feast and Famine as Revealed in Dreams,* became a classic in its field and sold over 10 million copies.

Joseph was a member of the cattle and wheat exchanges and a fellow of the Egyptian Academy of Clairvoyance.

He is survived by his wife and children, and several brothers.

ISRAEL: MOSES DIES AT 120, PARTED RED SEA

Moses, one of the pioneers and great leaders of Israel, died here today at the age of 120.

Moses was adopted by the Pharaoh's daughter when he was but an infant. An early champion of civil rights for the Hebrews, Moses, in his youth, severely beat and killed an Egyptian soldier who was mistreating a Hebrew slave. He was exiled to Midian, where for many years he labored as a shepherd. With the guidance of his patron, God, Moses negotiated the controversial release of the Hebrews from Egypt, and led them into the wilderness. It was on Mt. Sinai that he and God wrote the celebrated document, "Ten Commandments," which helped unite the people of Israel and for which they earned the Nobel Peace Prize.

In the arcane world of plagues and miracles, Moses had few equals.

The government of Israel has declared a day of fasting to observe his passing.

An official telegram from the Pharaoh was received this morning by the family, which reads: "Though we had our differences, I have always maintained respect for Moses. He was a great leader, and a formidable and resourceful opponent."

JERUSALEM: KING DAVID DEAD

David, former King of Israel, was found dead in the palace late last night. Royal physicians said the king died of natural causes.

David was much loved and respected by his people, ruling over Israel and Judea for some thirty-three years, before turning over the throne to his son Solomon.

A fighter in the mold of Muhammad Ali, David will probably be remembered best for his surprise hand-to-hand combat victory over the Philistine giant Goliath of

Gath, during the reign of Saul, and his little victory dance afterward on Goliath's head.

Aesthetically inclined, the ex-king spent his last years studying droll limericks with his seraglio.

JERUSALEM: SOLOMON DEAD: WAS WISE RULER OF ISRAEL AND JUDEA FOR FORTY YEARS

Solomon, the wisest and wealthiest of Israel's rulers, died yesterday of complications following a vasectomy operation.

Solomon was respected throughout the kingdom for his astute and often innovative restructuring of government, i.e., dividing Israel into twelve districts, each with an officer responsible to one chief. Many called him Israel's answer to Robert Moses. Solomon will also be remembered for his bold solution to the mind-body problem.

During his reign, Solomon married the daughter of the Pharaoh of Egypt, which helped cement relations between the two countries. The king counted among his personal friends and admirers the Queen of Sheba, King Hiram of Tyre, and numerous other leaders and dignitaries from around the world.

Solomon's only known vice was his legendary appetite for idol-worshiping women, of which he married some seven hundred.

In his spare time, Solomon was in inveterate composer of songs, having written a thousand and five, and proverbs numbering three thousand.

Following a private funeral service at the palace, burial will take place in the city of David.

Shrink Strike

Negotiators for patients and their psychiatrists intensified efforts yesterday to negotiate a new contract and avert a psychiatric strike threatened for Monday.

Representatives from each side conferred early in the day with Jules Luckincup, mediator in the dispute, and briefed him on the issues. Mr. Luckincup then analyzed the issues as best he could without dreams or slips. They involve demands for a fee increase of fifty dollars a week, greater job security, and Mr. Luckincup's need to send eggplants dressed in clerical garb to his friends and associates. The average psychiatrist's salary at present is only $250,000 per year, hardly adequate to support their sailboats, beach cottages in Martha's Vineyard, and ex-wives in today's inflationary economy.

The current contract is between the National Union of

Treatment or NUT, representing the more than 30 million patients in this country, and the American Psychiatric Association, local 26B. The pact expires midnight on Monday.

Meanwhile both sides are planning for a strike if there is no agreement. The APA said pickets would be on duty in front of all three thousand couches where it has jurisdiction if the talks fail. It said it expected the picket lines to be honored by Primal Screamers, EST trainers, flotation tankers, TM people, and all other therapists who might inadvertently be tempted to lure APA patients away during the strike.

The lieutenants of NUT for their part have made plans to deliver emergency services to those in need. Couches will be set up free of charge in the home-furnishings sections of major department stores where security analysts from leading brokerage houses have pledged to stand in as best they can.

Hundreds of sympathetic youth organizations have offered their best Tijuana Tea and liquor companies, booze, in place of traditional sedatives and antidepressants. And even known gossips have volunteered to run consciousness-raising groups until the strike is settled.

A spokesman for NUT calls the demands of the APA "crazy" and urges members to remain calm during the period or if necessary to lock themselves in closets.

The APA feels the patients are being unreasonable and resistive in blocking their demands. One particularly sensitive member of the APA's crack negotiating team put it this way: "You have to understand that these people from NUT are like children. They are acting out aggressive fantasies of feces retention. Sooner or later, though, the pressure will become too great and they will break, they always do."

At the moment the two sides appear to be far apart at

the bargaining table, and there is a lot of free-floating anxiety in both camps.

Some observers speculate that if the APA members would allow the team from NUT to sit at the bargaining table rather than lying supine on the floor, some of the difficulties might be stemmed. It has also been suggested that if the APA replaced the strict Freudians on the team, who only acknowledge points made during free association, further progress could be made. Of course, in fairness to the APA, the NUT members' tactics of shrieking, screaming, and panicking to gain the floor have not added to the productivity of the meetings. Nor have the little depressions and tantrums helped, especially the one by the nuclear scientist who held a cobalt bomb above his head and threatened the destruction of the world if he did not get his way. Six tranquilizer darts had to be fired before order was restored.

Mr. Luckincup, who is doing a yeoman's job, given the circumstances, says he intends to put before the bargaining teams a proposal involving fee payment on best efforts. Essentially this would mean a one-time large payment after a cure was effected.

Dr. Werner Schnitzel commenting on this possibility said, "Vot? Iss you crazy or somesing? I vant ze payment in advance. Vot insurance have ve got that ze patient von't flush himzelf down ze toilet just to avoid paying us? Ten years hard vork down ze toilet in a tvinkling. Never! (*sic*)"

The talks are scheduled to continue round the clock until a settlement is achieved. However, should the patients remain firm in their resolve, or get well, a settlement would become unlikely. In this unfortunate eventuality members of APA local 26B might deem it worthwhile to consider the merits of going into otolaryngology or plastics.

A Frinker
by Any
Other Name

March 1, 19—

Dear Mr. Frinker:

I have received your letter urging me to support Senate Bill 7057, legislation to increase the fees charged for licensing dogs in the City of New York.

As a longtime supporter of measures that ensure the humane treatment of animals, I will give careful consideration to your view favoring its passage during the current legislative session.

Thank you for writing to express your concern.

Sincerely,
Walker P. Gordon

Dear Senator Gordon,

Thank you for your letter of March 1, indicating your support for humane treatment of animals and your willingness to consider a yes vote on Bill 7057 which urges an increase in the fees charged for licensing dogs in the City of New York.

> Sincerely,
> Lewis B. Frumkes

P.S. My name is Frumkes, not Frinker

Dear Mr. Frinker:

Thank you for your most recent letter acknowledging receipt of my letter of March 1, which indicates pretty clearly I think, that I will carefully consider your "view" favoring the passage of Senate Bill 7057, not that I will consider voting "yes" on the bill itself. There is a distinction, you see.

> Sincerely,
> Walker P. Gordon

Dear Senator Gordon,

While your latest letter takes great pains to clarify your position vis-à-vis Senate Bill 7057, which I have urged you to vote yes on, it has not yet gotten my name straight, which is Frumkes, not Frinker. I don't quite know how to explain to you how Frinker sounds to someone who is actually Frumkes, but perhaps it would be roughly equivalent to my calling you Gorgon instead of Gordon.

> Sincerely,
> Lewis B. Frumkes

Dear Mr. Frinker:

I can only assume that your substitution of the name Gorgon for Gordon in your most recent letter is a harmless Freudian slip and not an intentional slur or attempt to link me in deed with one of those snake-headed ladies of old who on whim would turn people to stone. That said, allow me to reassure you that I have duly noted your feelings regarding Senate Bill 7057 which authorizes an increase in the fees charged for licensing dogs in the City of New York. Dogs, I might add, bear no resemblance to serpents.

Yours sincerely,
Walker P. Gordon

Dear Senator Gordon:

It strikes me as curious that you so sensitively misread my illustration of Gorgon for Gordon to make clear how I feel about Frinker for Frumkes, yet fail utterly to correct that error in letter after letter, namely that you address me courteously and correctly as Mr. Frumkes, not Mr. Frinker, which sounds uncomfortably similar to Fink and Stinker. Thank you for your attention in this matter.

Sincerely,
Lewis B. Frumkes

Dear Frinker:

Now that's about enough! To call a State Senator a fink and stinker after having suggested that he is no better than a snake, is pure insolence. I do not know

what motivates you, perhaps it is a temporary derange-
ment of some sort, but I do not wish to hear from you
again. The only reason that I even dignify your letter
with a reply is to teach you some manners. Good Day!

Senator Walker P. Gordon

P.S. For the record I plan to vote against Bill 7057 when
it comes up.

Dear State Senator Gorgon-Walker:

You insult Medusa by taking her name. In my opinion you are not even fit to clean her terrarium, much
less to wear the badge of State Senator. My dog, Gordon,
has left something appropriate for you in front of your
office downtown. When you step in it, do not, in your
wildest imagination, think it will bring you good luck.
Think rather that it will bring you more of the same
unless you vote yes on Bill 7057.

Yours,
Lewis B. Frinker

Frumkes' Rules of Order

The effect of an amendment may be obtained by calling for, or moving, the previous question or a different set of the pending questions (which must be consecutive and include the immediately pending question), in which case the vote is taken first on the motion which orders the previous question on the largest number of questions.

*A*bove, one of Robert's Rules, which some people had complained they had difficulty understanding. This struck me as odd in that these rules are couched in a clarity matched only by certain obscure sections of the tax law.

Nevertheless, last week, in a fit of creative energy, I decided to improve upon Robert's Rules, until then the standard for parliamentary procedure throughout the

English-speaking world. I set about this task not so much because Robert's Rules were no longer valid, as that people observing them began making perpetual motions, long sought by physicists, but deemed unacceptable among parliamentarians.

In this regard, while I retained much of the corpus of Robert's Rules, I provided important innovations that could not have been envisioned by Gen. Henry M. Robert, even if he were still around, or any other member of the big-brass military. I also alleviated almost all of the existing motion congestion and confusion by introducing the following practices.

Blurting

Blurting is the sudden or inadvertent uttering of a motion or question which arises usually spontaneously and of itself. It allows for heady cross fire and relief of pent-up frustration, which frequently attends convened assembly. Members are each permitted two blurts per meeting, and a careful count is kept by the secretary.

Interrupting

Hitherto, interrupting was looked upon as rude, crass, if not with disdain, by die-hard Robert's Rulers. In a bold break with tradition, I have made interruption a legitimate means of point making.

Interruptions may come at any time during the meeting except during a blurt in progress. Interrupting a blurt is considered out of order, and is punishable by cancellation of the interrupter's unused blurts. Members all have unlimited interruptions.

Reclaiming Canceled Unused Blurts

The interrupter whose unused blurts have been canceled may reclaim the unused blurts by soliciting a two-thirds affirmative vote from the assembly, or by punching out the other members. If the punching-out option is selected, the interrupter seeking vindication must notify the assembly of his intention, giving weaker members a chance to flee. Should the fleers effect a quorum, the interrupter is automatically vindicated and his unused blurts restored.

Blurting on an Interruption

While the interrupting of a blurt is punishable by cancellation of the interrupter's unused blurts, the converse is not true. Members may blurt on interruptions at will.

Interrupting an Interruption

Interruption of an interruption is considered bad form, as it tends to snowball, forcing the chairperson to resort to bullwhipping. It is, however, permissible.

Bullwhipping

Bullwhipping is the sole prerogative of the chairperson and is to be used only when an interruption of an interruption has snowballed into general chaos. At this point the chairperson may take the bullwhip and mercilessly flog the members until some semblance of order is brought about, and control by the chair is reestablished.

Methods of Obtaining the Floor

Often it is difficult for the individual member to obtain the floor, especially during periods of excessive blurting, snowballing interruptions, or bullwhipping. At these times two methods may be initiated to secure the attention of the members present.

LEAPING

Leaping requires that the member whose desire it is to obtain the floor leap from his seat over the table and onto the floor. He may then give a Tarzanlike shriek, or eructation, to further announce that the floor is his.

SHOUTING

The second, though less preferred, method of obtaining the floor is shouting.

In this procedure the member must bellow in stentorian tones one of several prescribed phrases:

Phrase 1.   Hey! I've got the floor.
Phrase 2.   Listen up, you guys.
Phrase 3.   Hold it down, please!

Emergency Procedure

If the floor cannot be obtained by either of the preceding methods, there is a third alternate procedure, to be used only in dire emergency. The member wishing to secure the floor may borrow from the arsenal of the chairperson a Valium bomb, which he holds above his head while exhorting the assembly to quiet. On securing the floor, the member must return the bomb to its place in front of the chairperson. Failure to replace the bomb is deemed sufficient cause to adjourn the meeting impromptu, or on occasion permanently.

Alternate Means of Adjournment

Adjournment under circumstances other than the Valium bomb option or unanimous vote may be achieved in several ways:

1.   A gradual attrition of members present resulting in an empty hall.
2.   A liturgical finale following an excessive bullwhipping by the chairperson.
3.   An emptying of the hall because of toxic levels of flatulence.

Applying for the Job

Dear Don Corleone,

Word is out that you are looking for a new lieutenant in your family ever since the unfortunate result of the tug-of-war last Thursday between your former lieutenant, Carmine Profiterrole, and the IND subway train bound for Jamaica.

With your permission, Don Corleone, I should like to apply for the position.

Enclosed is my résumé and a photograph of me posing with the chief engineer of the IND subway train. I am the one on the left holding out the stack of fifties, and he is the one on the right hiding his face from the camera.

Thank you for your consideration in this matter and I look forward to hearing from you at your earliest convenience.

Respectfully,
Linguine Aldente

RÉSUMÉ

NAME	Linguine Aldente
ALIAS	"The Sailor," "Uncle Knobs," "Riviera Harry," "Larry Fruit," "Goppo"
ADDRESS	Unknown
EXPERTISE	Garotting, bookmaking, leg-breaking, management

WORK EXPERIENCE

1981–1982	Associate lieutenant—Garbacho Mafia family—Bronx, N.Y.
1979–1981	Assistant lieutenant—Garbacho Mafia family—Bronx, N.Y.

Responsible for:
—liaison between consigliere Joe Wisdom and lieutenant Rocco Gorgonzola.
—personal hygiene of 115 soldiers, 3 drivers, 36 free-lance button men.
—preparation of agendas for intrafamily strategy meeting.

1979–1981 (cont.)	—prepared authorizations of expenditures of $175,000 budget. —prepared quantity audits, projections, and financial statements for numbers, loan-sharking, vice, narcotics, and gambling operations. —provided on-the-spot translations of dialect curses, names, and execrations.
1974–1979	Soldier—Garbacho Mafia family—Bronx, N.Y. —collected outstanding debts from garment salesmen, bars and restaurants, longshoremen. —set up MX-type mobile bookmaking system which became the prototype for other bookmaking operations around the country. —recruited new soldiers from: prisoners doing time, reform-school dropouts, illegal aliens.
1970–1974	Free-lance button man —carried out contracts for syndicate families as well as wealthy individuals. —taught Garotting at the New School for Social Research in N.Y.C. and Killing for Fun and Profit at The Education Exchange.
MEMBERSHIPS	Cosa Nostra

	Fellow—The American Society of Button Men Wire and Shiv
AWARDS	Soldier of the Year—1976 Golden Garrot—1972
RECORD	
1968–1969	San Quentin—paroled, good behavior
1962–1967	Alcatraz—armed robbery
1958–1961	Sing-Sing—extortion
EDUCATION	P.S. 147, Bronx, N.Y. St. Luke's Reform School—scholarship student
RECOMMENDATIONS	Don Ponto Garbacho c/o the Garbacho Mafia family Bronx, N.Y. Asst. Warden Harry Stiltskin Alcatraz Penitentiary San Francisco, Calif.

Letters of Recommendation

RE: THE LONE RANGER

Dear Sirs:

Lone is a shy sort of guy (he wears a mask) who prefers individual effort to group participation. As such, he is not exactly an organization man and is considered a little strange by peers. On the job, however, he is an efficient and exuberant worker who gives a little yell, "Hi yo Silver, away!" whenever he completes an assignment successfully. Last year he gave two hundred of these little yells and was invited to join the "Million or More" club.

I think he will make a fine addition to Metropolitan Life's sales force.

> Sincerely,
> Tonto Cooperman
> Former partner

Dear Sirs: Heeeerrrrrr's Johnnnnny!

I am writing on behalf of Johnny Carson, who has applied for the position of guest host on his own show. In that guest host must really show up and cannot be replaced by a guest host once removed, Johnny is asking for $3,000,000,000 in salary and all the outstanding stock in NBC.

I think you should give Johnny what he wants, since he is far and away the best talk-show host on network television, and owes a lot of money to two brothers in Bayonne named Knobs and Mr. Fruit. If the job is not forthcoming, Johnny will have to assume the role of Aunt Blabby on rather a more permanent basis. Besides, what would Ed McMahon do without him? And Doc, and Tommy, and the whole gang? Give Johnny a break.

> Sincerely,
> Grant Tinker

Dear Sirs:

I am happy to be writing a recommendation for my good friend Field Marshal Idi Amin Dada, President and Officer in Charge of the Gumball Machine for Life, The Republic Of Uganda, Emeritus.

As you probably are aware, Idi left Uganda shortly after a heated philosophical disagreement with the present government who stated publicly that it wanted to set a small nuclear device off in his mouth. It was Idi's feeling that other suitable sites could be found.

Jolly, shrewd, occasionally lucid; these are some of the many qualities that make Idi one of the most charismatic and sought-after leaders in modern history. Without reservation, I heartily recommend him for the position of chief butcher at the B & D abattoir.

Sincerely,
Yasir Arafat

Dear Sirs:

I am writing to you about Superman, a.k.a. Clark Kent, or as he is still known in certain circles from his days with the criminal justice department, "Old Krypton Face."

Superman is without doubt one of the most remarkable men to have ever flown with a cape. He is faster than a speeding bullet, more powerful than a locomotive, able to leap tall buildings at a single bound. He is invulnerable to bullets, as tenacious as twenty oxen and considered almost as smart. In my judgment he will make an excellent fullback with the Steelers' offense.

Sincerely,
Lex Luthor

P.S. Should he not work out for any reason, you can always sell him to the Hughes Tool Company as a drill bit.

Dear Sirs:

As a dear friend of Henry Kissinger's I would like to tell you why I think Henry would make a good waiter in

your restaurant. First of all Henry is very smart and
very international. He would never mix up orders. How
many other waiters know the difference between natur
schnitzel and schnitzel a la Holstein? Or Sacher torte
and Sacher Von Masoch? Not many. And Henry has a
sense of history. He would steep himself in the early
lore of the restaurant, study old menus so that he could
regale the patrons with stories and imbue them with a
sense of trust. But best of all Henry is a superb negotia-
tor. If, for example, a disgruntled diner felt he was being
overcharged on his meal and refused to pay, Henry
could negotiate a deal. Perhaps the outraged patron
would not have to pay for the unused portion of his dinner. Instead Henry would arrange for a steep bread tar-
iff or borscht tax. One way or another he would make
sure the restaurant got its due. Henry is a master at
such things—I should know. All in all I think you
would do well to hire Henry in your restaurant. Just
make sure there are no pretty waitresses near his station.

Yours,
Richard Nixon

Dear Sirs:

I am writing to you on behalf of HRH the Prince of
Wales and Lady Diana Spencer, the now Princess of
Wales, in reference to your ad in the paper for a live-in
couple.

HRH advises me that he and his lady would be happy
to live in your home for the tidy sum of £12,000 per
month, thereby conferring upon you and your family
great social distinction and cachet. You would make no
demands upon the royal couple and would refer to them

at all times as HRH and Lady Diana, though for an extra thousand pounds you may privately call him "Chuck" and her "Cute Stuff."

There is little question that they are the best possible couple for this position.

> Respectfully,
> Lord Conklin Stiltskin
> Duke of Worcestershiresauce

Dear Sirs:

I am writing in support of Brooke Shields for Commissioner of Education. I believe that Brooke has something special that others in municipal government do not. Admittedly, some may have more brains, and others more experience, but none, to the best of my knowledge, brings to public service their Calvins. Brooke can also contort her body into unusual positions, which none of the other candidates seem to be able to do. Surely this must count for something.

> Sincerely,
> Gloria Vanderbilt
> for Murjani

Dear Sirs:

I have known Muhammad Ali intimately through his ventriloquist, Howard Cosell, for the last ten years.

When he is not "whupping" opponents in the ring, or trapping roaches on TV, he can be found attending to his favorite philanthropic pursuits, such as "Ali for king", "Forever Ali" or stretching his mouth in the mirror.

When he has regained the heavyweight champion-
ship of the world for the 840th time, and finally retires,
I am sure he will fit into your company perfectly as an
air-raid warden. Also, do me a favor personally, will
you? Tell your employees to call him "Clay."

Sincerely,
Joe Frazier

Too Busy Going to the Job to Make Any Real Money?

*T*hink you've got problems, right? Wrong. My name is Frankie Pistol and I remember when a bank turned me down for a $200 loan. Now I lend money to the bank— certificates of deposit at $100,000 a crack, sometimes more. Best of all, it's their money.

I remember the day a car dealer got nervous because I was behind on my payments and repossessed my car. Now I own a Rolls-Royce, banana cream and salmon. I paid $43,000 for it—cash.

I remember the day my wife phoned me, crying, because the landlord had shown up at our house demanding rent, and we didn't have the money to pay it. He even turned down my wife's offer to lie bound to the railroad tracks humming theme music from "The Perils of

Pauline," her favorite erotic fantasy. How humiliating!

Now we own six homes. Two are on the oceanfront in California, similar in feeling to the old Nixon villa in San Clemente. Two are posh condominiums overlooking secret lagoons in Florida. And two are tropical getaways strategically located somewhere in the Caribbean.

Right now I could sell all my property, without touching any of my other investments, and walk away with $3 million. But I don't want to sell, because I don't need the money. I've got other real estate—and stocks, bonds, gold, cash in the bank.

How did I do it?

Bank robbery, that's how. Sure you may say, "Bank robbery is illegal; it's all right for him to rob banks, he got away with it. But I don't want to spend the rest of my life in jail."

And that's the point, my friends. You don't have to spend the rest of your life in jail. At most you may have to do five, maybe ten years, depending on whether or not you get caught and which state you live in. What's five years if you don't smoke compared with the remainder of your life living in the lap of luxury?

I remember when I lost my job. Because I was head over heels in debt, my lawyer told me the only thing I could do was declare bankruptcy.

He was wrong.

I bumped off my creditors one by one. Now I'm not suggesting you do that. I offer it only as an illustration of how creative force can be used in the service of desperation.

Now I have a million-dollar line of credit, more if I need it; but I still don't have a job. Instead I get up every weekday morning and decide whether I want to go to work or not. Sometimes I do—for an hour; that's all the average bank robbery takes. But about half the time,

I just loll on the beach, do "Shuffle Off to Buffalo" a few times, or some pratfalls, and go back to sleep. That's why I call bank robbery "the lazy man's way to riches."

I know what it's like to be poor, scratching at a neighbor's doorstep for a few pennies. And I know what it's like to be rich beyond my wildest dreams; to have yachts, racing cars, and beautiful women falling all over me, to never have to ask the price of pizza.

I know that you, like me, can decide which it's going to be. It's as simple as that.

So I'm going to ask you to send me something I don't need, as a token of good faith. Ten dollars. Why? Because I want you to pay attention. Studies have shown that people pay more attention to things they have paid dearly for than things given them for free. Once you've plunked down ten bucks I figure you'll look over what I send you and decide whether to send it back or keep it. And I don't want you to keep it unless you agree that it's the best advice on bank robbery you've ever received. In fact, I won't cash your check until after you've pulled your first heist. How's that for a guarantee?

I know what you're thinking: "He got rich telling people how to rob banks." The truth is—and this is very important—five years before I shared "Bank Robbery— The Lazy Way to Riches," my income was $660,000 from just four small banks in the San Diego area. And what I'll send you tells you just how I made that kind of money, working a few hours a day, twice a month.

It doesn't require "education." I'm a high school dropout. It doesn't require "capital." Remember I was broke when I started. It doesn't require "luck." No bank robber is lucky. And it doesn't require "youth." One old gizzard I worked with is over eighty. He's traveled the world over, making all the money he needs, doing what I taught him.

What does it require?

Belief. Enough to take a chance and absorb what I send you. Nothing more.
You will learn:

Principles of planning.

Staking out.

How to tell a "full" bank from an "empty."

The ins and outs of alarms.

Twenty different notes you can hand the teller—all proven—including the classic THIS IS A STICKUP and four others that will show you are above all a "gentleman."

Means of egress: i.e., the getaway car, the subway, the feet.

How and where to bury loot.

How to throw police off your trail, Bloodhounds.

Your rights if arrested.

The names of a dozen attorneys in your area who specialize in defending bank robbers.

Penalties for bank robbery in each of the fifty states.

Lamaze techniques for whiling the time away in solitary.

If you follow my instructions carefully, the results will be hard to believe. In fact, one of my former students, a "lifer," reputedly has $2,000,000 stashed away somewhere for when he gets out. Hard to believe, right? Right!

Here is what others have said:

Made $16,000 First Time Out

"The first bank I hit, a small one in Omaha, I made $16,000. Most of it was in Susan B. Anthony dollars. That's great results first time out, right?"

P.P.M.

Omaha, Neb.

Everything We Want

"We can't keep this to ourselves any longer. You were right. We're on the road to riches. Traveling cross-country, we have hit fourteen banks for a total of $560,000. It was a piece of cake. We now have five Cadillacs and a helicopter for spotting."

Mr. & Mrs. T.R.M.
On the road.

What I'm telling you probably runs contrary to what you were taught by your pastor, teachers, friends, and family. But ask yourself this question: How many of them are millionaires?

And finally, allow me to share with you some wisdom from a major Italian philosopher, Al Capone, who once said, "A kind word and a gun will get you further than a kind word."

These simple words, carved in the forehead of an old friend, have been inspirational for me, and I hope they will be for you too.

Frankie Pistol

Run, Run, Run

I'm told I run like the wind, invisible, swirling and eddying, going "whoooo, whooooo," admittedly an unorthodox style but one well suited to my temperament. It was not always so. Just five years ago I weighed 320 pounds, which the doctor said was too much for my five-foot, two-inch frame. I was out of shape. I used to go "whoooo, whooooo," but it was from the bedroom to the bathroom. Then I discovered running, and it changed my life.

Running obsessed me and I ran with passion and panache, though more often with passion as the panache weighed heavily and slowed me down. Muggers returning from work would smile and wave to me and I would nod back in acknowledgment. Soon I was easily running hundreds of miles per day and, as my speed increased, I began to take running leaps from state to state, seldom bothering to exchange currencies as I didn't remain in any one spot long enough to warrant it. On a recent jog around the country I was picked up as a UFO by no less then ten states and given fighter escort back home.

Of course, there are many reasons to run other than health. Running is an excellent way to unload the tensions of the day, unless you run into a pole, which is nature's way of telling you that you are too relaxed. Running also improves your looks, which is important if you are not a hermit and like to interact with other people. Many runners tell of huge gains in interacting after they have taken up running. In fact, the astonishing rate of divorce among runners is probably attributable to excessive interacting.

Like most sports, running carries with it certain considerations that must be taken into account before one begins. If you are over eighty-five and prone to coma, you should look to other forms of recreation. Rocking, for example, provides a wonderful sense of movement without endangering your health and doesn't slow down other participants. Nor should you run on an empty stomach, especially if it isn't your own. You should have a complete physical before running. Occasionally a runner comes out to run sartorially resplendent in Gucci shorts and Maud Frizon track shoes. He does a little ritual dance as a warming-up exercise before running and drops dead. Had he been smart, he would have worn old shoes and a sweat suit.

Because of my unique style, that of running like the wind, I am often called upon as a consultant by track teams and fugitives. Thus, running has become something of a vocation for me, and there are little tips I give to my clients which may prove valuable to any of you who are thinking of running. I offer them here only as suggestions.

1. Always try to alternate your feet when running. Hopping may be chic, but it is also exhausting.
2. Soak your feet in lemon juice before and after running. This prevents athlete's foot and also makes them taste better.
3. Never run after a mechanical rabbit.

It is probably clear by now, even to the dullest of you, that, like a clock, running has become part of me. I am afraid to stop.

Highlights of the Great International Film Festival and Cook-Off

DINDIDINDIDIN SHANKAR WOW!
(GONE IN A FLASH)
INDIA 1983

Highly acclaimed at both the Bangalore and Cannes festivals earlier this year, *Dindidindidin* examines the fragile yet volatile relationship which develops in the jungle between a lonely untouchable and a ten-foot Bengal tiger. Using special red filters and industrial cotton, director Mrinal Drumjar takes great care to depict the final, tragic scene, where the tiger loses patience with Gita, tastefully and with a minimum of gore.

Running time—1 min. 30 sec.

RIK TOI TOI IGLOO
(IGLOO MARY)
ESKIMO 1983

Toi Toi (Mary), the ingenuous heroine of Popo Bon Ton's first venture into pornography, is a bored igloo-wife who has affairs with Jon Joi, a fisherman of no special celebrity, then with a penguin, then Jon Joi again, then an iceberg, then the penguin again, penguin, penguin, penguin. Filmed in stark and unrelenting black and white, Bon Ton pulls out all stops on this unusual look at pent-up passion and obsessive love in the frozen wastes.

CING PIAO
(FIVE BOWLS OF RICE)
CHINA 1983

Director Rory Foo loses no time introducing us to Peng, the reluctant hero of this Kafkaesque tale about a school-boy who wakes up one morning and discovers that he has turned into an egg roll. Foo explores the psychological implications of transmogrification; what it means to be a normal, healthy adolescent, and then suddenly, without warning, a food. We explore with Peng the initial shock of the transformation, his gradual resentment and anger at being an egg roll rather than a main course such as Peking Duck, and finally his acceptance of the new condition. Is Peng as egg roll a metaphor for life? Director Foo leaves us in a veritable state of metaphysical tumescence as the film ends.

Winner of the prize for most peculiar script—Cannes Film Festival 1983

86

Das Vidanya KGB
(KGB Farewell)
U.S.S.R. 1983

Pushpin is a ranking KGB agent in Moscow. Things
start to happen when Pushpin meets Vasily, a double
agent for British Intelligence, known as 008 & 009. Vasily has in his possession plans for a new Soviet missile
which can effectively elude all Western defenses. Why
does Pushpin take a certain liking to Vasily and forget
about the plans? Why does he follow him around like a
puppy dog and shine his shoes and carry his briefcase?
Is it Vasily's dark good looks, or is it the villa on the
Riviera stocked with naked women and caviar and fast
cars, plus £2,000,000 sterling in a Swiss bank account
that Vasily has promised Pushpin? While we never learn
for sure, it is a safe bet that it is the villa on the Riviera
and the £2,000,000 sterling. Sash and Ivan Bobka are a
tour de force as Vasily.

Running time—12 hours 36 min.

Thump Thump
France 1983

Bravely extending the limits of cinema pedophilia in
the tradition of *Lolita, Sundays and Cybele,* and *Beau
Pere,* director Bertolt Bleu sensitively portrays a young
man's tragic seduction by a precocious fetus. Their only
means of communication being a fetal monitor at the local
hospital, Tammy (the fetus) and Rene gradually come to
realize the star-crossed futility of their love. The film

triumphs through its honesty and delicate handling of a touchy subject.

Prize for special effects—Black Forest Film Festival

Il Noodle Multo Longo
(The Longest Noodle)
Italy 1983

Filmed in and around the famed tortellini works of southern Italy, *Il Noodle Multo Longo* is about two rival chefs who make a wager as to who can make the longest unbroken strand of linguine al dente. During the contest, Gino, played by Bronzini Castello, adds Elmer's to his batter, while Angelo loses interest and pursues the saucy Celestina who clops him over the head with a frying pan. Good fun in the magnificent Italian pasta country.

Order of Merit—Unionale Di Pasta

The Social Clime

*P*alm Beach, that fontanel of soft living, was the setting last weekend for the annual Palmball Cotillion, which benefits learning-disabled crustaceans and others of that ilk. Mrs. Cherryblossom Wheelock—she's the former stripper and wife of Bangkock Wheelock, the onionaire— gave a little cocktail party for two thousand before the evening's festivities got under way. Count de Noir, who made a fortune in garlic during the vampire scare in the fifties, flew in from Transylvania just after sunset. The Garlock Humpits of Chattanooga were there, as was Mrs. Howley Woodclover who motored down from her puppet ranch in Sarasota. Cuffy, Puffy, and Muffy Wheelock looked like angelic little gorgons as they sashayed across the family gardens, which were tented over in midnight-blue hopsacking to match the starlit sky. By ten o'clock, the lilting strains of the "Melancholy Sarcophagus" had died down and the guests were spirited away to the cotillion by a mobile armada of sequined horse-drawn Black-Marias, supplied for the occasion by the Skullduggery Corp., one of Mr. Wheelock's far-flung enterprises. Kudos to Cherry Wheelock and her busy little beavers, who always find time for worthwhile causes despite their hectic schedule of entertaining and shop-hopping.

You may have guessed it, that sweet little thing seen around town on the arm and in the pants of debonair, ageless Count Ormani Vilani (his grandfather invented pizza) was none other than Sissy Sinkworth, daughter of Horace Sinkworth and Princess Cordovan Die Schneerwall of Bayonne and points south. Wedding bells?

The Met opened last night with its new production of *Soirees de Beignes.* On hand for the opening were Ambassador Hildebrand Von Orphiluxen, Mr. and Mrs. Sorce Foxencloak, Didi Dufois, Senator and Mrs. Hobart Cantilever, Mayor Jack Dort, and other luminated celebraries too supernumerous to mention. After the performance, a late supper was held at L'Incroyable, hosted by the effervescent Mrs. Loy Bushman, the antacid queen. Among the late diners were Dowager Annie Von Dusen Mishnaldrick, escorted by World War I hero "Dogface" Copely, Hope Redux, looking radiant in her bright orange chiffon netchkin and wearing her famous ruby pilaster tiara, Basil Stiltskin, Capulet Redunsky with Dame Goiter Kiswel, and Cesarine Holyoke, one of those remarkable seven sisters. From L'Incroyable the late revelers moved to Orpheus, the new after-hours discotheque located under the Seventh Avenue IRT.

Dancing the "Hummingbird" in a corner with Eurydice Beamish was Rear Admiral Dunston Cornhall, taking time off from his arduous duties as Chairman of the Joint Chiefs of Staff. Sitting at the Admiral's table, sipping champagne and prune juice, were other military dignitaries, including SAC head General Lobo Conitz and his lovely wife Ariel, Mark Thyme of the C.I.A., and Secretary of Defense Carl "Hothead" Andrews.

Speaking of the military, Sarah Jean Tushwell, of the Newport Tushwells, will sponsor a bash this week at La Fedidite, her villa in Cannes. The afternoon banquet will be followed by organized games of backgammon, karate, and pin-the-tail-on-the-donkey. Guest of honor at the fete will be martial-arts mavin and international bon vivant, Carlos Le Doight.

There is a rumor circulating that a certain party is seeing a certain party.

Michael Forsquin, the developer and owner of Club Onan, has announced the opening of his new year-round resort on Easter Island. It will feature indoor and outdoor croquet courts, two restaurants, one serving continental cuisine, the other deli, a quatrefoil swimming pool filled with Perrier water, and suites boasting sunken onyx bidets and video tape machines. If you have to ask, you can't afford it.

Film mogul, Paedophilia Scava, and fourteen-year-old tennis star, Millie Moskowitz, have broken their engagement. She played the lead in his last film, *Confessions of a Tennis Buff.* Paedo, as his friends call him, escorted twelve-year-old Okie Anderson to the premiere of *Rover Gets His Bone,* which opened last night at the Civoli Theater.

If oil man Punch Larkin has his way, and he usually does, the $10 million which he donated to Houston Cultural Center will be used to build the largest marionette theater in the world. Punch recently returned to his eggplant farm from a hunting safari in Africa, where he bagged several gazelle with his custom howitzer. On his return from Africa, the oil magnate's wife Judy presented him with a twenty-fifth anniversary gift, a life-size marionette of himself. C'est la guerre.

Thought for the day: For the rich they sing.

Aerobic Typing

Unless I miss my guess, you would probably prefer movie-star looks and robust good health to being dead. Most people do. That is why I have written *Typing Your Way to Movie-Star Looks and Robust Good Health* for Pernicious Press, $14.95.

In *Typing Your Way to Movie-Star Looks and Robust Good Health* I discuss how typing can transform you from your present state of "yuck" into a new person, one radiating well-toned muscles and inner confidence. I will show you, for example, how typing the letter "e" 320 times per minute for only four hours a day will increase your cardiovascular fitness and harden your finger at the same time. You will be able to punch holes in cardboard, wood, plastic, all but the toughest steel, using nothing but your fingers. I don't know about you, but in the past I always had to use a hammer and chisel to open my crate of oranges from Florida—now I use my finger. In fact, around our house one can frequently hear people at work or on the terrace calling "Hey! Get the finger."

But a finger-tool is only one of the benefits to be derived from typing; cardiovascular fitness is even more important. Hearts and lungs, like other muscles, must be exercised to become strong and to make us less vulnerable to heart attacks and strokes. Aerobic exercises such as acute anxiety are one way to condition these organs, but not all of us want to hyperventilate on a regular basis. Typing provides a safe, easy, and interesting way to exercise your organs right in your own home. It also burns three calories an hour. You can work off a piece of cake in just two years.

If going the cardiovascular route, you will want to get your heart rate up to about 50 percent of its maximum capacity if you are thirty years old; 75 percent if you are thirty years old and athletic; or 110 percent if you come from above 96th Street and take long walks at night. You will also want to sustain this rate for at least a month.

The best way to begin is to go slowly at first, pecking with two fingers and using gentle words and sentences until you are comfortable with the keys and have learned the basic rules of "white out." After a few weeks of "hunt and peck" you may move on to "touch" and some simple annoying phrases. Your mother-in-law's name or "Damn! another bill" will suffice to increase your heart rate. Before long you will find yourself attacking the keyboard with letters to the editor, sex novels, and memos to the IRS. Your heart will beat new and interesting rhythms in your chest.

Naturally there are certain considerations you will want

to take into account before beginning a serious typing program.

1. *Check with your doctor.* Make sure your heart can stand the awful strain of seeing your words in print. Make sure the doctor can stand the strain of seeing your words in print.
2. *Choose your typewriter carefully.* In most cases it is the typewriter that is responsible for what you say. You must choose between an electric and a manual. The electric can go faster, but a manual will require your heart to work harder. Make sure the typewriter can stand seeing your words in print.
3. *Other equipment.* Will you be using corrasable paper so that you can erase errors, or liquid paper? If the latter, be sure to order industrial size in kegs. Make sure your seat is uncomfortable so that you won't fall asleep. Ideally you could sit on a pin.
4. *Have something to say.* Without something to say you will be sitting in front of the typewriter like a dummy. Many famous writers have nothing to say and wind up working for ventriloquists.

A final note. When you take up aerobic typing (typing above 150 words per minute), whether for fun or for movie-star looks and robust good health, it is important not to overdo. One aerobic typist, 600 WMP, got carried away and typed two thousand letters to the Department of Health protesting the cholesterol count. When no reply was forthcoming, she tried to commit suicide by eating her own words.

Another woman who had typed eight hundred pages

of highly polished manuscript in fifteen minutes suffered a mild ink fit and was hospitalized for three weeks.

Rare though these incidents be, they point up the need, as with any conditioning program, to begin slowly and work up to the desired goal.

END OF EXERCISE—REPEAT FOUR TIMES

Willard's Words

W. W. *Willard*, the celebrated author, critic, playwright, and raconteur, will put his entire vocabulary up for sale next month at the Sotheby Parke Bernet Galleries. Yesterday's announcement of the auction caused a widespread stir among collectors and wordsmiths both here and abroad, and the three-day sale is expected to attract a large attendance.

What the public is bound to find remarkable about the Willard offering is the enormous range and quality of the collection. It is common knowledge that W. W. Willard has assembled one of the largest and most complete idiomatic vocabularies in the English-speaking world, but it may come as a surprise to many that he also possesses the finest set of seventeenth-century French expletives outside the Library of Congress, and a hitherto unknown collection of Tibetan humor words.

Mr. Willard speaks glibly and openly about these, but denies that he ever acquired the French expletives for use other than in polite conversation. As for the Tibetan humor words, he says, "I've always liked Tibetan humor, it is under-appreciated here in the West."

Irwin Armpant, Sotheby's resident lexical specialist, predicts that many of the words in the Willard vocabulary will set record prices. Of particular interest should be the extremely rare words of praise Willard employed during his stint as literary critic for the *Boston Barnacle*. Words such as "okay" and "amusing" are estimated to bring between five and eight thousand dollars each, while the "terrific" used to describe Sylvia Kronish's *Eggplant Time* may fetch in excess of fifty thousand, according to Armpant.

At the auction, Mr. Willard's vocabulary will be divided by period, chronologically, for purposes of simplification. Thus on the first day, lots 1–200 will include words from infancy through latency, while lots 201–500 will take in those from secondary school and university. Officials in charge of the very early words, which are listed in the catalogue under "Goo and Gah," have already received hundreds of mail bids from child development specialists and mothers around the country. The evening of the first day of auction will feature words from Mr. Willard's army experience, noted in the catalogue as "*#%)@?." Mr. Willard regards this colorful group as the "backbone" of his speaking vocabulary, without which he will be virtually tongue-tied. Philosophically, he muses "what the . . . !" and adds, wistfully, "shoot!" Persons attending the "army" sale will be required by Sotheby to furnish identification proving that they are over twenty-one, or from culturally deprived backgrounds.

On the second day, lots 501–2002 will come on the block. Here the connoisseur will be able to find words and phrases culled from Mr. Willard's extensive travels and political harangues. Memorable lines such as "Hi, how're you," and "How's it goin'?" will be spotlighted. Not to be overlooked on day three are Mr. Willard's personal favorites, words he reserved for use with close friends and relatives, "C'mon," "Get off it," and "You're something!" to name a few. If the Willard collection is nothing else, and there are some who feel that way, it is rich in the clank and fire of the descriptive adjectives for which Willard is justly famed. "Beautiful," "hairlike," "dunky," and "cute" spring immediately to mind.

For those with more exotic tastes, there is the full complement of "Willardisms," words coined by Willard himself, and by Barney Bomglass, who sometimes wrote under Willard's name. Here one may find "flaggeline," "gumpet," "doodecker," and "miclymate," all words which helped shape Willard's reputation as an eccentric and which are contained in the "Ecce Willard," his impassioned self-celebration.

Those who attend the preauction exhibit at Sotheby's will see most of, but not all of, W. W. Willard's vocabulary set out on framed 2″ × 4″ note cards. Willard has retained several words which he feels will be necessary to negotiate the rest of his life. Not for sale are the words "help," "bathroom," "food," and "ouch."

Willard says that the decision to sell virtually all of his spoken and written vocabulary had nothing to do with financial distress. Rather it was the result of his desire to become unencumbered from a lifetime of words and devote his remaining years to the pursuit of silence. His philosophy, he says, "grew out of a mature and personal conviction that Wittgenstein was correct when he said,

'Whereof one does not know, thereof one must be silent,' or something like that."

Whether W. W. Willard can, as he vows, give up language and live in the monastic style he has prescribed for himself is doubted by those who know him best. What is not in doubt, however, is that the words he sells at Sotheby's next month will never ring the same.

Met Given
$10 Million
Drug Collection

A drug collection rich in tranquilizers and antihistamines and valued at $8 to $12 million will be given to the Metropolitan Museum by a New York addict, Stephanie Melisande Bombadier. The entire collection will be exhibited at the museum next fall.

Mrs. Bombadier's holdings include several hundred modern medicines and thirty or forty examples of primitive drugs such as Dewars White Label, Thunderbird, and Elmer's Glue.

The agents were described yesterday by Marcel Blitzkrieg, the Metropolitan's director, as "a pioneering collection, one of the great collections of contemporary medicines in the United States, and the single greatest in terms of sedative tranquilizers, hypnotics, and antidepressants." Continued Mr. Blitzkrieg, "They add an important new dimension to our own holdings in twentieth-century pharmaceutica, which have been severely depleted in recent years due to increased anxiety and higher pollen counts."

After a long period of abuse, the Met has organized its drug department and slowly rebuilt its collection with the aim of making it equal or strategically superior to any other in the world.

Asked why she had donated the collection, Mrs. Bombadier said, "I felt the museum needed a shot in the arm. This was my way of providing it."

The gift, which has been variously described by pharmacists as "magnificent" and "hot stuff," includes bottle after bottle of rainbow-colored Valiums, Libriums, Dalmanes, Tranxenes, Ativans, Azenes, Seraxes, Miltowns, and Equanils all taken by Mrs. Bombadier during her hyper-anxiety attack of 1950–1965. Other stars among Mrs. Bombadier's tranquilizer acquisitions are Thorazines, Mellarils, Tuinals, Quaaludes, and Mogadons. This latter group are numbered multiples in series of 2 to 4 billion stamped by the pharmaceutical companies that made them. Certain other mood-altering drugs and antidepressants such as Lithiums, Stelazines, Compazines, and Haldols also caught the fancy of knowledgeable druggists and users.

ANTIHISTAMINES

Outstanding antihistamines by major domestic producers include Actifeds, Allerests, Benadryls, Chlor-Trimetons, Coricidins, Dimetapps, Dramamines, Phenergans, and Triaminics, as well as a very early bottle of Dristan which is half empty and considered exceedingly rare.

The primitive group includes several "Rye and Gingers" circa 1957, which Mr. Blitzkrieg said were virtually unobtainable today, a full array of hobby airplane glues, and a sealed bag of bus fumes from central New Jersey.

The sixty-eight-year-old Mrs. Bombadier, a one-time addict, acquired the bulk of her collection over a lifetime devoted to the medicinal arts. A frequent visitor to drug emporiums both here and abroad, she counted pharmacists, easy prescribing doctors, and anyone else who could get her drugs among her friends.

Buying drugs at a time when most people were unaware of their myriad uses, Mrs. Bombadier paid prevailing prices for them. The heroin in her collection, for example, now valued at $3 million, was purchased for $300 in 1951, and the "Good Grass" now worth about $1.5 million was acquired for next to nothing from a Mexican upholsterer who was using it to stuff chairs.

Mrs. Bombadier was one of the first to recognize and acquire Kaopectate for use other than as window caulking. By 1955 she is said to have formed the most significant group of tranquilizers in private or public hands and was using it to seduce geese. "Her taste was unusually relaxed," said Guy Fixx, chairman of the department of twentieth-century drugs at the Metropolitan. And he recalled a remark by the famous dealer Carmine Peter Green, who sold Mrs. Bombadier her later works: "In acquiring drugs, she would invariably use her American Express card rather than cash and code words such as 'sleepy' and 'peppy' and 'dopey.' "

Although she has had many purchase offers in recent years, especially from "young people" and "big eyes," Mrs. Bombadier said, "I never considered selling the drugs, because to me they were the moon and the stars."

Mrs. Bombadier, the former Stephanie Crusthammer,

is married to Colefax Bombadier, the well-known Rhinoplast and polo player. She built most of her collection she says from her husband's "nose money."

Mrs. Bombadier has been named an honorary trustee of the Met, and at a dinner last week in her honor she laughed and said, "I'm high as a kite." The question remaining in everyone's mind is, who will get her cosmetics?

Looking for La Creme de la Crude

*B*reathes there a red-blooded American, old enough to have a driver's license, who at one time or another hasn't asked him or herself, is American oil really as good as the best oil of Arabia? Does anything measure up, say, to Saudi Arabian oil? Is it possible to do a completely objective blind testing and find out? Unlikely, but I decided to try anyhow. I was aware that too many variables exist to obtain total objectivity, which would explain why some oils rank high at one testing and low at the next. Oil A may seem better when burned before oil B, while oil B may react strangely in the engine when blended with Chivas Regal twelve-year-old, or "zip," the additives used to give extra power. Temperature may also be a factor. Arabian oils seem to like dry desert heat, while New York State and some of the smaller New England crudes prefer cold. And there are those users who can tell the probable origin of an oil even when every effort has been made to hide its identity; they can tell by the "nose" and the way it "combusts."

Nevertheless, over the years, certain oils consistently score well, largely because they are refined with great care and devotion and because they come from fields ideally located to take advantage of sedimentation and soil conditions. In this category are only a handful of the most celebrated oils of the Persian Gulf, oils whose reputations have preceded them across the globe.

Probably the best known of these is Saudi Arabian Reserve, the oil that was ranked first in the OPEC classification of 1973, and the oil that has been fetching record prices at auction, the ultimate oil man's oil.

No American oil can match the reputation of Saudi Reserve, but several domestic crudes produced in Oklahoma and Texas and a light shale from the Gulf of Mexico are beginning to attract large followings because of their great style and quality. Any list would have to include certain grades from Standard Oil of Miami, Atlantic Richfield VFOP (very fine old petroleum), and Amerada Hess Off Shore, not to mention the reserves of Getty and Texaco.

These are produced in modest quantities and are expensive because they represent the best grades from the most capable wells in the Southwest. They are pumped from the same rock and sand that are found in the Persian Gulf countries and the refining techniques in both places are similar; so any comparison is valid.

Are they as good as Saudi Arabian Reserve? An unusual opportunity to judge presented itself recently when a group of exceptional petrophiles gathered in New York for an afternoon of motoring and camaraderie.

Among those present were Alice Lampskin, oil columnist for *Fortune Magazine* and author of *Things Move*

Better with Oil; Jack Snuff, national president of the So-
ciété des Pétroles; James Berry-Hill, curator of the Bic
Benedek Oil Museum in Dallas; and Anthony LaMode, a
teamster and gasoline buff.

I purchased single barrels of Saudi Arabian Reserve
1974, Saudi Reserve '75, Standard Oil of Miami Special
Reserve '74, Atlantic Richfield VFOP '75, Amerada Hess
'75, and Getty and Texaco reserves '74.

I chose Saudi Arabian Reserve from two wells in an
effort to achieve fairness. The 1975 was an infinitely better well, but at least a decade away from maturity, though
it will never achieve the greatness of the '74.

The wells of '74 in the Southwest were excellent, so
comparing them with a mediocre well from the Persian
Gulf would not be fair. Comparing them, however, with
the '74s and '75s would be appropriate.

Testing the Saudi Reserve blind against a group of
American refined and shales would constitute fairness.
The goal was to select not only the best oil of the group,
the one that burned best at the moment, but the one that
also showed promise of further development.

Here then the results:

The Standard Oil of Miami Special Reserve '74, was
clearly the winner, garnering more votes than any of the
other oils. Tied for second were Atlantic Richfield VFOP
and the Texaco Reserve. Third and fourth, respectively,
were Saudi Arabian Reserve '75 and Amerada Hess '75.
The Saudi Arabian '74 finished fifth.

Several of us could easily identify the Saudi oils from
their bouquet, which is distinctive, especially in a closed
room. But the '74 lacked the depth and texture of the
Standard Oil and the '75 was too young. There is little
doubt that it will fare better in comparison five years
hence.

Here are my testing notes. The oils are listed with their
per-barrel prices, in the order of the consensus.

Standard Oil of Miami Special Reserve '74, $34.95

Musty but rich bouquet redolent of shale. Big. Full and smoky in the burning, although young. Full of hydrocarbons. Deep and black. Stylish.

Atlantic Richfield VFOP '75, $15.95

Rich shale bouquet, but closed. Elegant but slightly viscous. Stylish but undeveloped smokiness.

Texaco Reserve '74, $16.99

Light sedimentary bouquet. Slippery. Not big. Closed in and smoky. Ungenerous. Good texture, not watery but hydrocarbons are hidden. Good potential.

Saudi Arabian Reserve '75, $200.00

Tight but classic young Saudi bouquet, full of currency. Rich green, but ungenerous. Lacking in hydrocarbons. Slightly viscous. Unyielding.

Amerada Hess '75, $17.50

Very rich, musty shale bouquet. Big nose. Hydrocarbons aplenty. But neutral, not big. Hollow.

Saudi Arabian Reserve '74, $150.00

Very developed bouquet, but pale green. Unripe and thin. Still young but should peak in two or three years.

It will be said that the testing did not prove American oils superior to Persian Gulf oils. That what was demonstrated was only that one particular group of experts preferred certain domestic oils to the great Saudi Arabian Special Reserve on one particular day in New York. The same testing held later in the week, month, or year, might produce entirely different results. Quite frankly, I doubt it.

Research Indicates Cars May Talk

*T*wo scientists from the General Motors Laboratories in Ann Arbor, Michigan, have found evidence that some automobiles do indeed use a rudimentary language to communicate with other vehicles.

Incredible? Yes and no. According to a report by Robert M. Lintdrummer and Pierre Aujour D'hui in the *New England Journal of Driving,* compact-sized vehicles in particular make sounds that can only be interpreted as a rudimentary language. The researchers added that they expected their findings to be disputed by other mechanics and automotive engineers.

In their experiment Doctors Lintdrummer and Aujour D'hui worked with two Volkswagen Rabbits named Hansel and Gretel. The Volkswagen named Gretel, and referred to as "liebchen," was trained to identify the colors red, green, and yellow by tooting her horn at the appropriate color light. Hansel, meanwhile, was taught to name a color by flashing his headlights. Correct answers were rewarded with fresh oil.

Training complete, the Volkswagens were united in a double plexiglass hangar for testing. At first they just idled alongside each other, sniffing exhaust pipes, as autos newly met are wont to do. But soon Hansel initiated conversation by flashing his headlights in the configuration, "What color?"

Gretel, irritated by the question, mimicked him, "What color? What Color?"

Hansel repeated the question, "What color?"

And Gretel replied correctly, "Red," but in a sarcastic tone.

Hansel flashed his grill at Gretel in what could only be construed as a broad smile. Gretel steered her front wheels away from Hansel and rolled her headlights up into her hood in mock exasperation. Hansel flashed again, "What color?"

And this time Gretel began to backfire in rage. But finally she tooted the correct answer, "Green." One technician swears that later in the evening in response to a question by Hansel, Gretel answered something about a "hoodache," but this could not be confirmed.

Doctors Lintdrummer and Aujour D'hui believe that this experiment proves, once and for all, that cars can and do learn to talk. However, Tony Potswain, chief wrench at the A & D Body Shop in South Orange, disagrees sharply with the doctors' conclusions, dismissing the Volkswagen demonstration as a reductio ad absurdum. Mr. Potswain contends, "Dere was probably some little midget under da hood working dem lights and horns. C'mon, who da ya think you're foolin'? Cars can't talk."

As with any controversial research there has been much lively debate recently over the extent to which compact cars can be taught artificial language in the laboratory. One precocious Honda Civic, last year, was reputed to have uttered 360 primary words to a favorite technician. Unfortunately the technician has refused to reveal the content of what was said, claiming it is a personal matter. She is presently being tortured at the GM labs and a spokesman for the huge automobile company says a statement is expected early next week.

How do Doctors Lintdrummer and Aujour D'hui account for the compact car's apparent ability to acquire language?

"In primitive times," say the doctors, "compact cars are thought to have roamed the plains in small packs, attacking stray buses and vans for gas. We must assume that the first cars spoke a very simple and restricted tongue, unlike any natural language of today." The "first-of-all" language would not show verb phrases, or pronouns, or adjectives. Just simple forceful locutions such as, "Ummmm," "truck," "gas." Only later would the phonetic and grammatical elaboration that we take for granted have become manifest.

Of course, this is by no means the only theory that claims to account for the origins of automotive language. Other postulations range from the belief that car language arose through the imitation of animal noises, especially the imitation of geese (the so-called "honk honk" theory), to the belief that language is the outcome of a random biological event or mutation.

In Bethesda, a researcher has documented separate signals among cars to warn of fire engines, potholes, and radar traps. There is also a distinct call for humans crossing the street which is similar, for some reason, to the signal for potholes. One theorist speculated that perhaps humans look like potholes, but this line of reasoning has not caught on. Many machines seemingly have ways of spreading the word when danger approaches. Air conditioners, for example, go phtttt sputtt when the temperature rises above 105° Fahrenheit, and TVs in trouble go on the fritz. It is just that automobiles appear to do it with unusual semantic precision.

Hitherto, the ability to convey messages that carry specific information content had always been considered a distinguishing feature of human speech. Scientists are no longer sure. If cars can communicate, what about lamps, and washing machines, and, God forbid, vacuum cleaners?

A Guide
to the
Lesser Sheiks

SHEIK ABDUL EL FAZIZ Y COCOBLANCAS

*B*y far the richest of the lesser sheiks, Abdul El Faziz y Cocoblancas of Kuwait and Hallendale, Florida, has a daily oil income twice the gross national product of Mars, not including outside investments in real estate and securities or royalties from his best-selling book, *Abdul's Complete Book of Sand.*

Sheik Faziz y Cocoblancas is known to be wise, he owns a piece of the rock; brave, he eats his mother-in-law's cooking; and handsome, he bears a strong resemblance to Nanook of the North. However, he is not much of an athlete and prefers spending his time at home, hanging around the seraglio with his favorite odalisque, Herpes.

SHEIK FAHD EL DOONEY

Small and inconsequential, Fahd El Dooney of Oman made a life decision early on to renounce the trappings of decadent Western society, fine champagne, jets, fast cars, and wild women, and to become a servant of the people. Because of his self-sacrificing philosophy and ascetic ways, El Dooney is looked upon with great respect by his fellow sheiks who call upon him frequently to take out the garbage. Uncertain as to whether or not he made the right decision, Sheik El Dooney can often be found kissing the toes of the other sheiks and begging to be beaten or used as a doormat. He is in treatment thirty-five times a week with a strict Freudian analyst.

SHEIK ACHMET EL MAMOUN

Before his promotion to sheik, Achmet El Mamoun, which means "son of ranch fossil" in Arabic, was chief flog for the South Yemen police department where he developed the now popular Middle-Eastern technique of whipping miscreants publicly to the tunes of "Get Along Little Dogie," "Moon Over Miami," and "On Wisconsin." "On Wisconsin" was his particular favorite.

An early devotee of bizarre S & M, Sheik Mamoun came close to losing his life in the spring of 1974 when a camel he was beating turned on him and bit off his fishnet stockings and most of his garter belt.

SHEIK MURRAY COHEN

Sheik Murray Cohen of Abi Gezind, a settlement on the West Bank, is not exactly a sheik in the strict sense of the word, though he does drive a Seville and hand out five-dollar tips to the barber, manicurist, and shoe-shine boy at Mohammed's hair-styling emporium every Tuesday.

What he really is, is "chic," says his wife Muriel, who thinks he looks stunning in his new beige and white leisure suit which she gave to him on the occasion of his fifty-ninth birthday last July. God knows he has enough ties and cuff links.

SHEIK YAMANI TURKI IBN WORKING ON THE RAILROAD

In the world of the lesser sheiks, no one is considered lesser of a sheik than Yamani Turki ibn Working on the Railroad, whose main claim to fame is his 2 percent interest in the old turban works at Abu Kemal. Sheik "ibn Working," as he is called by his friends, believes strongly that head coverings are coming back and recently spent a week in Texas trying to sell the Dallas Cowboys on the idea of using turbans instead of helmets. Catching onto the concept quickly and impressed by all he was trying to do for them, the Cowboys used "ibn Working" as a tackling dummy in five successive workouts. Microsurgeons from Baylor University Hospital and a special team from London have spent the last three weeks trying to piece the sheik back together again.

If the surgery is successful, it is thought the sheik will most closely resemble an old shoe in the years ahead. Sheik "ibn Working" thanks Allah that he didn't try to sell turbans to the Redskins.

SHEIK SAAD SAAD SAAD

There are sheiks and there are sheiks, but this one is
Saad Saad Saad. No matter where he goes people say,
"That is Saad Saad Saad" and wag their heads from side
to side as if to say, "Saad, Saad, Saad." In the final analysis, there is not much to say of Sheik Saad Saad Saad
other than that he is Saad Saad Saad and leave it at that.

Coup Coup
in the
Seychelles

Victoria, the Seychelles, often confused with an excellent Buitoni pasta product, was taken over today by two mercenaries with sticks. President and Field Marshal for life, Big Daddy Boo Vons, whose pro-Western government was overthrown and who escaped from his tree house to London, had this to say about the coup: "Abi doubi dabi awisa swaili malli abi doubi zoubi goobi," and then commented acerbically, "Doubi abi abi zoobi goobi mali swaki mali abi zoobi!"

Radio Seychelles, a CB, announced that Prime Minister Harold Mowgli, in the name of the mercenaries, had taken control of the islands and that anyone venturing into the streets would be cast in bronze and left unsigned.

The Seychelles, long a bastion of totalitarian viewpoints and way station for Hasidim visiting the Indian

Ocean, has been a hotbed of steamy political unrest much of this decade. Throughout its volatile history the island has been divided by factions seeking to gain control of its principal industry, the export of butterfly wings. Butterfly wings, which are an essential ingredient in witches' potions and Brut, are plucked under careful supervision of government inspectors and packed in glassine envelopes for shipment to covens around the globe.

In capitals of the world, reactions to the Seychelles coup have been mixed. President Mitterrand in Paris issued a statement to the effect that he has always enjoyed seychelles, while in Bonn, Chancellor Kohl said, "Und de zaben griben gutten himmel" and fainted. There were concerns in Washington that the Kremlin had trained the stick-wielding mercenaries of Prime Minister Mowgli, known as Frick and Frack, and that the Soviets were seeking the Seychelles for use as a KGB picnic site. Reports supporting these fears have been leaking out of the nearby Comoro Islands, where hordes of pink-tinged and even red butterflies have been sighted. Secretary Shultz has ordered all foreign aid to the Seychelles temporarily discontinued, pending clarification of the Mowgli government's official intentions.

A leader for the powerful lepidopterist lobby in Washington has called on the Reagan administration to ban all imports of butterfly wings to this country and further suggests that the government put pressure on the Seychelles to allow live flies to leave. The lobby has been joined in this plea for civil rights by the gay liberation movement, who actively support freedom for all winged creatures.

The manner of the coup, that of taking over a country with sticks, has caused a stir among political and military observers both here and abroad. It is believed the sticks were of ordinary wood, as were the mercenaries; and if this be true, how then were the mercenaries able to accomplish the coup without warning and with such relative ease, especially since the Seychelles army is known to be well trained and mean? The answer may lie in the rebels' having spoken softly and carried big sticks, but this is only speculation. Another theory holds that the rebels were disguised as two traveling Franciscan pole-vaulters in the process of island hopping, but this too is merely conjecture.

At present, Big Daddy Boo Vons is seeking to recruit mercenaries and butterfly fetishists in Soho and Picca-dilly for the purpose of retaking his islands, about which he feels strongly. Failing this, he plans to open a video arcade.

While capturing the Seychelles with sticks is without precedent, and annoying, it has its compensations. There may usher in an era of bloodless revolution in which commandoes with sticks replace atomic weapons. After all, what good is an atomic bomb or even a cruise missile in hand-to-hand combat? Above all, business and com-merce should benefit. Already Remco and Mattel are pre-paring "coup sticks," and other toy manufacturers are looking ahead to "coup kits." As these kits proliferate there may be danger ahead, much as FDR foresaw the danger of a chicken in every pot, but kept it to himself.

For the time being, there is little likelihood of a Sey-chelles-type coup happening in the United States, what with security in Washington eclipsing even that of 744 Park.

Exotic Gifts from Larry & Harry

#95

ROYAL IMPERIAL VALIUM
AMERICA'S FAVORITE
TRANQUILIZER—
ONLY BETTER

*L*arry and I could talk our heads off but we can't say a thing that sounds half as fine as the effect these tranqs will have on you. So unusual, not one person in a thousand has ever experienced them. That's because your doctor can't prescribe them and your druggist can't slip them to you under the counter. These egg-sized beauties, weighing 50,000 milligrams each, were made up special for us by the pharmaceutical company that invented them. Each one is like a little atomic bomb of pleasure. This long-remembered gift makes you long-remembered as a thoughtful, original gift-giver. In fact, the individual whom you gift with Royal Imperial Valiums will probably hound you the rest of your life for more.

Order Gift #95 Royal Imperial Valium $18.95 delv'd
Special 50 Royal Imperial Valium
   in wicker basket $99.95

#812

TABLETOP-CAGED SWEDISH DWARF COMPLETELY DRESSED—LIVING AND FRESH THE UNUSUAL GIFT

Natural North Woods beauty in a perfectly formed, live, miniature Swedish dwarf, from Sweden. This apple-cheeked symmetrical dwarf is already four years old and over 8 inches tall—comes precaged and completely dressed in Swedish country troll suit.

And wait until your friends see it, asmiling and as-pouting untranslatable Swedish execrations as it jumps up and down in its authentic gold-colored metal cage, just atrying to get out. A gift they'll enjoy during the holidays, on special occasions, or any other time of the year, dwarfs have no season; and come warm weather this hardy trouble-free dwarf can be hung in the yard as a living sculpture, or set among the shrubs as a squirrel-watch. It adds that magic touch the day it arrives. Ideal for mantel or tabletop, kitchen or guest room, the children's room or Grandmom's foyer.

Perfect delivery guaranteed. Food pellets included.

Order Gift #812 Swedish Dwarf $21.95 delv'd

#12

FRESH PIRANHA CAVIAR
THE RAREST DELICACY
OF THEM ALL

Ever since the Ayatollah instructed Iranian sturgeons to stop laying, gourmets everywhere have been searching for the better caviar. Larry and I think you'll agree that fresh piranha caviar is not only the rarest caviar in the world (no one has survived to taste it yet), but also the best. At great expense we have sent our divers into the Amazon wearing three-ply-steel-belted armor to bring you back this most exotic of delicacies. Each exquisite little pearl of an egg will delight your sense buds as no other caviar has—careful though, if one seems to be hatching, in which case you'd better make a run for it.

Order Gift #12   Piranha Caviar   @ $100 per oz
            "   Fresh   @ $1,000 per oz

#758

OUR OWN SHOOTING FUDGE
WITH SYRINGE
TRIPLE SEC CHOCOLATE
—DIRECT PLEASURE

For all you chocolate addicts who have always wanted to shoot it up, now you can. Shooting fudge is a veritable symphony of the finest chocolate made in our Mount Ogiwa bakery, with only half the clogging power of cholesterol. No lumps or clots here. Created especially for us by wild Nigerian chocolate elves, shooting fudge can entertain the entire family for days on end. Or try it in an I.V.— let it drip into your system slowly and delectably as you lie by the fire reading limericks or listening to soft music.

Order Gift #758 Shooting Fudge $14.95
Extra Syringes   @$1.95 each

#45

SPECIAL DELUXE GRAB-BAG

Control of any two nations for a period of one week. Choose from Armenia, Chile, England, France, Iraq, Mauritania, Norway, Poland, Spain, Turkey, Yugoslavia, or Zaire.

Plus

A million dollars a week for life or a two-bedroom co-op on the Upper East Side of Manhattan. Not both.

Plus
Guaranteed seating at Elaine's restaurant on either the twenty-third of March at 10 P.M., or the seventeenth of July at 4 P.M.

Order Gift #45 Deluxe Grab-bag $115

#540

THE MERCEDES-BENZ GLIDER
STATUS AT A PRICE

Larry and I know that most people out there in Giftland would like to drive a Mercedes-Benz automobile just like all the brokers and lawyers, if only they could afford one. And why not? A Mercedes-Benz car bespeaks status and class. It confers upon its owner the recognition he so richly deserves for having a minimum net worth of $50,000, or in the case of a lease, $1,300 per month income.

That is why Larry and I have made it possible for you to give this gift of class for only $5,900, tax included. The Mercedes-Benz Glider is indistinguishable from other top-of-the-line Mercedes autos, unless you happen to look under the hood—in which case you are in for a big surprise. But studies have shown that most Mercedes owners never do look under the hood, so only their garage mechanics will know for sure.

Order Gift #540 Mercedes Glider $5,900 tax included

Cuba Libre

*F*or some time now I have been planning to invade Cuba, in part because I perceive United States security to be threatened by the presence of a hostile totalitarian state so close to our shores and also because I am low on Havana cigars. My invasion, though, will not be another fiasco like the "Bay of Pigs"; rather it will be a carefully planned operation, for if nothing else I am a perfectionist in such matters and there are many who feel I am nothing else.

In preparing for my invasion I have made a detailed study of the island so as not to confuse it with Canada or New Guinea. I have determined that Cuba is the largest and most populous of the West Indian islands included between the meridians of 74°7' and 84°57' west longitude and the parallels of 19°48' and 23°13' north latitude. It divides the entrance to the Gulf of Mexico into two passages of nearly equal width—the Straits of Florida, about 110 miles wide between Capes Hicacos and Arenas in Florida, and the Yucután Channel, about 130 miles wide between Capes San Antonio and Catoche. On the northeast, east, and southeast, narrower channels separate it from the Bahamas, Haiti, and Jamaica. It is also populated, I have learned, by Cubans.

Physically, the island is long and narrow, somewhat in the form of an irregular crescent, or a regular pheasant, my advisors are not sure. In any event, the north littoral, characterized by bluffs, becomes higher and higher toward the east, rising to 600 feet at Cape Maisí. The bluffs are marked by distinct terraces, and it is here that I intend to land. I shall accomplish the landing by means of a rented Goodyear blimp, which will be painted brown and bear the inscription, UPMAN, MADE IN HAVANA. This is sure to fool the Cubans, who will think it is an enormous floating cigar, or the detritus from a large bird. The blimp will be chock-full of crouching commandoes, highly trained in karate and pinching, who will be wearing sneakers so as to ensure the covert nature of our mission. The stratagem you may recognize as a modern version of the old Trojan Horse gambit, employed successfully by the Greeks during the Trojo-Graeco war.

From Cape Maisí, it will be a relatively simple matter to traverse the island to Havana where we will camp out in the Caves of Cotilla, assuming there are no bats. If all goes well, we shall enter the capital city of Havana sometime after sunrise the following day, disguised as a group of foraging land crabs, which are numerous on the island and not likely to arouse suspicion. There is a remote chance that we could be discovered, and if that were to occur, it would be wise to avoid eating crabmeat exported from Cuba for at least two months. But we do not anticipate any problems in that direction and fully expect to secure the capital by nightfall. It is the boldness of our plan and the element of surprise which should work to our advantage. Once the island is under control of the "Cigarillo Liberation And Movement," or CLAM as we refer to ourselves, I shall proclaim myself Field Marshal and set about the task of restoring Cuba to its former grandeur as a small insect-infested island south of Florida.

Bunny Burgermeister Loves Books

"*C*hrist," says Bunny Burgermeister reaching for a small volume on the third shelf, "this book is all about Christ, not the man, but the message, if you know what I mean? God, I just love books. I love the way they look all dolled up in their little dust jackets waiting to go out, and I love the way they smell fresh off the presses."

Bunny Burgermeister is sitting on a motorized ladder against a great wall of books, hanging on for dear life as he whizzes back and forth from one end of the shelf to the other. He stops now and again to fondle a De Maupassant or a Proust as if it were a long lost friend and extemporizes on why his new book emporium, Le Book, which he opened with cummerbund heiress Puff Perryweather, is such a success. Occasionally he stops to fondle Puff herself. He likes the way she looks all dolled up in her new dust jacket and the way she smells fresh off the presses. But his fondling of Puff is strictly avuncular, for she is without substance. The books, however, are quite another story, and he caresses them as he would a gifted child for whom he felt an abiding passion. Here in Le Book, in the privacy of his own commercial establishment, he is free to fondle the books to his heart's desire. It was not always so.

During the fifties he was arrested twice in Skyboro, in the little town in which he grew up, for book molesting and served time. Bibliophilia is little understood even today, but in the fifties it was considered especially heinous and perverse. Young Burgermeister was dubbed a "bib" and a "worm," and was reviewed with unkindness wherever he went. Once while visiting a library in upper Gardenia he was caught "bowdlerizing" a first edition of *Winnie the Pooh* between the racks and severely chastised. Had it been known that extra-illustration had also been done, there is no telling what might have ensued.

Bunny speaks of Skyboro and his years there in guarded terms as befits an ex-con smitten with guilt. He holds no grudges, but he does not feel comfortable with the idea that in this enlightened day and age foxing is still regarded akin to sodomy in most states.

"It is really amazing in how many different ways men get their thrills or kicks out of life," says Bunny Burgermeister sitting atop his ladder, for all the world a prince of his demesne. "There is, as I see it, no reason why a man should not amuse himself by expurgating a classic for his own amusement once in a while; the harm arises when he presumes to do it for the public at large. Yet is the church held up to scorn for its encyclicals? No. But when an individual is found expurgating in the privacy of his own home, an act as intellectually natural in its way as Godel's Theorem, he is held up to ridicule."

With this Bunny Burgermeister loses his footing on

the ladder and tumbles headlong into a pile of old *Partisan Reviews*. Regaining his feet at once he beckons me to follow him. We enter into a small, softly lit chamber in the rear of the store. "This is called The Nook, sort of the bibliophile's Plato's Retreat," he continues. "It is where our better customers come to be alone with their favorite books. Here there are no literary judgments made about choice or aspersions cast about the moral turpitude of the reader. He may indulge his every whim, be it only the gentle appreciation of a style or cover, or the hard-core physical contact of a lifetime's fantasy. Indeed, just last week two excited literary critics came here with a much praised first novel and spent two and one half glorious hours undisturbed. One can only surmise what may have transpired in the room, but when they left it was with satisfied smiles on their faces and fifty bucks to each of my salesmen.

"Another of my customers, an elementary school-teacher, has a penchant for reading books about the grave, ghoulish things that would stand your hair on end. She does not dare read them at home for fear her family would misunderstand. In fact, she once confided to me in private that during a particularly gruesome passage from *Death Knocks*, she climaxed no less than two dozen times. And she is hardly unusual. We have fine-bindings freaks who spend hours on hours sidling up to full morocco and calf, and then those who only enjoy staining vellum. One, shall we say, 'dirty old man,' but very rich, comes here just for little books, octavos and miniatures, that sort of thing, and never fails to thank me profusely when he leaves."

As we return to bookstore center, Bunny excuses himself for a moment to help one of the customers. It is a woman looking for a book to take her down from the manic phase of a shuttle neurosis. He suggests some Dostoevski followed by the complete Krafft-Ebing set to verse.

She should check back with him in a week. "These are my people," says Bunny. "They trust me. I am their doctor, psychiatrist, friend." He catches the ladder, which is still whizzing back and forth, and hops aboard. As he fades into the distance, his voice trailing off among the sections containing *Tall Homosexual Poets* and *Early Serbian Humor*, I hear the lilting strains of "Zookie the Bookie" coming over the stereo. Quick as a flash Bunny is back. He offers to show me his all-time best-seller, his own book, *The Bunny Book.*

"Over the years I've become friends with most of the writers. Salinger, Cheever, Updike; they're all my friends. So I got this idea for *The Bunny Book* in which I ask each writer to do a sketch of himself as a rabbit. At any rate, when I had collected about two hundred of these rabbit pictures, I put them together in *The Bunny Book,* and it has been selling like crazy ever since. Here, look at this one. Would you believe Groucho Marx smoking a carrot? Or Gore Vidal with whiskers? This is one of my favorites, Truman Capote in the middle of a hutch. He's the little cute one on the end with the rose sunglasses."

Bunny whipped out a Pentel and signed his name in a *Bunny Book.* "This is for you," he said with a wink and jumped back on the ladder. As I squeezed through the crowds pouring into Le Book I thought to myself, this is no dumb bunny.

The New Punctuation

As section chief with the Department of Words and Letters, I have been asked to develop a new punctuation more in keeping with today's usage.

To this end, I have studied the notation of music, mathematics, and West Indian bulb talk in order to come up with an appropriate representation. In addition, I must explain to the writing public, the people who will ultimately consume the new punctuation, the differences between, say, the "anti-pause" and the "babble," or the "stream-of-consciousness mark." Not an easy task by any means.

The purpose of punctuation, as I understand it, is to make the meanings of sentences unmistakably clear, something which I believe the new punctuation accomplishes.

If all goes as planned, these symbols, devices, and marks should find their way into the idiom, perhaps as early as next year. Here is a little preview.

LBF, Washington, 1983

The Halt—Stronger than a period. The halt signals an abrupt and serious stop.
1. I guess that's it, folks ☉
2. The next one who speaks is middle class ☉

The Crescendo—Used to show something is building, as anger.
1. If I have to tell you to sit down one more time, Sitzfleish, I'll explode
2. Here's Johnnny

The Delta-Sarc—indicates spoken sarcasm.
1. I'll just bet you do △
2. Brilliant, Harold, now what do we do △

The Sigh—Used to emphasize resignation.
1. Oh well, I guess so ꟼ
2. Isn't she magnificent ꟼ

The Answer Mark—Opposite of a question mark. The answer mark is used to indicate that a question is being answered.
1. Who do? You do ∠
2. How much is that jeebie? Twenty-five dollars ∠

The Diddledy Dot—The diddledy dot is used to indicate frivolity.
1. Oh ho, he makes $400,000 a year, does he

2. Sorry, didn't mean to walk in on you like that $_o{}^o{}_o{}_o$

The Anti-Pause—The anti-pause indicates that one should move on, not stop. May be sprinkled liberally around prose or poetry.

1. Don't stop here ⌒
2. Notice there are no stops ⌒

The Babble—Unlike the anti-pause the babble is not just used to indicate the absence of a pause but to show a run-on run-together pattern of writing or speech as I am doing here continuous nonstop.

The Stream-of-Consciousness Mark—The stream-of-consciousness mark is used to suggest pure unadulterated flow, as maybe I will or maybe I won't, gosh! she was pretty—I wonder when next I'll see her, you like music don't you? Of course you do—red, green, a window— there is hardly any connection between the thoughts or logic contained therein. Abadabadabadaba do doo.

A Word About Pausals

Pausals are used in place of knowledge to fill the gaps and ellipses in our speech. Because of the frequency with which they lace our discourse, they require symbols.

This is the symbol for "you know," by far the most popular of the current crop of pausals.

1.   I'd like to go **✗** , but I can't. **✗** how it is,
     , **✗** , if I could, I would, **✗**
2.   (An extreme case)

(This is the symbol for "uh," somewhat old-fashioned but still very much with us.

1.   Ladies and gentlemen, I'd, (, like to tell you a, (, few things about, (,the company.

⋈ The symbol for "agh," the lesser of the pausal weeds but the choice of some.

〰 **The Segue**—The segue is used to make elegant transitions, as from the middle of a sentence, paragraph, or piece to the end. Usually it is made with subtle prose; however, when the writer has nothing to say, he may substitute the segue.

● **The Fin**—The end. Finality. That's it baby.

Sending Parents Off to Camp

More children than ever before it seems are packing their parents off to summer camp and with good and sufficient reason. Parents, unrefreshed by a summer vacation, tend to get edgy and bored, grouchy and mean. They take their frustrations out on the kids. "Go to your room, Coxswain, and don't come out until you graduate from college." "Walk the dog, Sally. I don't care if you just walked him ten minutes ago, walk him again. Dogs have needs too, you know." "Sylvan, if I've told you once, I've told you a thousand times, your floor is not a hamper."

The real reason though, beyond the obvious, parents get on kids' nerves is that the office and the home can do only a part of the job of turning a parent into a confident, well-rounded person. A camp can fill in the essential gaps.

At summer camp parents learn to live away from their children socially, with others whom they can't boss around. They learn to share and to function in a group. They learn self-reliance, discipline, responsibility. They will develop new skills. Their sense of self and their sense of values will bloom. They will grow emotionally and build character. Not bad for a few weeks in the woods, right? Right. Except that not all parents immediately understand this. Some are reluctant to go to summer camp and must be gently encouraged.

Witness my own.

"I don't know, Son, your mother and I are not sure we want to go to camp this summer."

"Don't worry, Dad, you'll love it."

"You know we haven't played sports in years, we could injure ourselves."

"You won't, Dad, but even if you did they have a first-rate infirmary."

"Who else is going, Son?"

"All the other parents, Dad, everyone you know, the Marksons, and the DeLupos, and the Dripkins, they're all going."

"Do we have to go?"

"Yes, Dad, you do, but you're going to love it. You won't want to come home."

"Which camp are you sending us to, Son?"

"The best, Dad, Camp Run-A-Muck in the pines; that's where all your friends are going."

Dear Son,

Camp is everything you said it would be and more. We are divided into seasons according to our age. Thus the twenties and thirties are called Spring; the forties and fifties, Summer; the sixties and seventies, Fall or Autumn; and those above seventy-five, Winter. Your mother and I are part of the Summer season and are quartered in bunk #32, along with the Dripkins and the Butterchurns.

Phoebe Butterchurn is much more attractive in shorts than I would have imagined, though your mother thinks she looks like a frog. The other night Mom frenched Phoebe's bed and a little hair-pulling ensued until we men were able to separate the girls around five in the morning.

Have to go now, I'm late for swim. If you get a chance would you please send me a carton of Marlboros and a bottle of J&B? Neither of these items are sold in the canteen. Thanks.

Love,
Dad

P.S. Son, when you send the cigarettes and booze, please wrap them in tinfoil and mark "Medicine" on the outside. That's my boy.

If you are sending your parents to camp for the summer, you will have to decide what type of camp you want for them. Will it be a camp for losing weight—both of them would probably benefit from shedding a few pounds—or a camp for sailing, riding, or golf? There are also camps for parents with emotional problems, learning disabilities, drinking problems, and physical handicaps. And, of course, there are the general camps where parents can choose from a wide variety of activities suitable for their age bracket.

An important consideration, and one you may want to discuss with your parents in advance, is whether you will be sending them to the same camp or to different camps. There are, after all, camps just for moms, and camps just for dads. Some parents prefer a little respite from their spouses, if even for a few weeks during the summer, while others prefer to stay together, either from force of habit or true love. Whichever the case with your parents, it is wise to let them have some say in this matter so that they don't feel manipulated and resentful. Summer camp should be a refreshing and exhilarating experience for them, not a burden and a hardship.

Inevitably, at summer camp, some separations and divorce actions will occur, especially at camps which have no night patrol or where the softball competition is allowed to get out of hand. This is to be expected and in the long run is probably for the good of all. More than likely your parents will return together at the end of August, flushed with confidence and invigorated, so not to worry.

Should they return separated or divorced, however, it would be better to send them to a different camp next summer, or maybe summer school.

Despite what you may think, parents do enjoy the summer-camp experience. They grow in their relationships toward each other and they come home loving you more. And at summer's end if you were to hover over the banquet set out in the woods, you would hear three hundred parental voices singing:

> *Oh, Run-A-Muk*
> *Oh, Run-A-Muk*
> *How we love you*
> *In the pines.*

And if you looked more closely, you wouldn't see a dry eye in the crowd.

Preparing Easter Eggs for the Holiday Season

*S*pring is in the air and the Easter Bunny is jetting up from Aruba where he winters nowadays, preferring the scrubby divi-divi trees and tropical lagoons to the snow and ice of colder climes. I don't blame him. Here at home it is time to dust off our Easter baskets and start preparing eggs for the holiday festivities. No more mixing six colored dyes in bowls of water, and dipping the eggs until they are brassy shades of pink, and blue, and green, violet, and yellow. Today we immerse our eggs scientifically in a total program of physical fitness and cosmetic rehabilitation until they develop what you might call their own personas and are able to stand alone without decoration.

EXERCISE YOUR EGGS

One of the best ways to make sure your eggs are fit for holiday fun is to give them plenty of exercise. It will not only make them look better, it will make them taste and feel better as well. Always use an egg timer so that the eggs do not exceed their limits of endurance—three minutes is usually a healthy workout.

Caution: If you choose jogging for your eggs, be careful that they do not bounce too much—their yolks could scramble prematurely, causing them to feel sick or nauseated. Also, because of their shape, short and ovoid, eggs will sometimes cheat during a run by rolling down a hill or over a grassy knoll, defeating the whole purpose of the exercise, and, in the case of the knoll, risking a crack in the process. Remember, while cute, eggs are not smart and must be carefully monitored during any exercise.

Besides jogging, swimming is also an excellent conditioner for your eggs, though good judgment must always remain in force. One careless individual recently left her eggs in a pot to swim never noticing the high flame underneath. When she returned from answering the front door, in what seemed but moments, her eggs had been tragically hard-boiled.

Tennis, too, can prove dangerous for an egg. Only last summer a myopic player of no repute mistook his egg for a ball and sent it hurtling into the net at ninety miles an hour. The egg's shell was so badly mangled that not even all the king's men and all the king's horses, who happened to be in the neighborhood at the time, could put it back together again. Sadly, the egg fried on the net.

PUT YOUR EGGS ON A DIET

Nothing is so sloppy-looking or unappetizing as a fat, ungainly egg, one whose epicycle is real wobbly when set into motion on a table. Put your egg on a diet which will keep him appealing without causing embonpoint. Reduce his intake of mayonnaise and nog by surrounding him as much as possible with celery and carrot sticks, parsley and lettuce. If he has to snack, give him paprika.

DRESSING YOUR EGGS

When it comes to Easter there is nothing more important by way of preparation than dressing your eggs. This year the "in" fashion egg color is gold. All the rich, romantic associations we make with gold are poured into the best clothes right now. Gold is precious—it's opulent, it's hot, it's sexy. Think of the fabled goose. What did she lay? That's right, a golden egg. Dress your egg in gold. Gold slacks, gold blouses and shirts, little gold jumpers, dresses, coats, ensembles. Yes, even gold Zena jeans. There are more clothes to be had for eggs than there are for Barbie dolls. All the top designers are giving themselves over to making egg clothes. Ralph Lauren, Halston, Adolpho, Mary McFadden, Bill Blass, even Trigère.

Trigère, doyen of haute couture, is making egg clothes. And if she isn't, she soon will be.

Dress your eggs to suit your fantasies: Princess Di egg, S & M egg, Western egg, El Capitain egg, Space egg, Park Avenue egg, Co-op Board President egg, Reggie Jackson egg, Pac Man egg, Upscale Bank Vice President egg, Disco egg, Reaganomic egg.

Dress your egg to suit your parent's fantasies: Doctor

or Dentist egg, Junior Senator from Any Important State egg, Happily Married egg with three or four children, living in the suburbs, near them, or Retirement Village egg.

Dress your eggs to suit my fantasies: Free-lance Writer with Arab Sheik's Income egg, Porsche-driving egg with Rolex Watch, or in a lesser fantasy, Honda Civic-driving egg with Timex, Black Hole egg Drawing a Bead on an Infinite Pizza, Hugh Hefner egg (Sultan egg, Emperor egg, or Pharaoh egg may be substituted at any time for the Hefner egg), Personal Friend of Snoopy egg.

EAT YOUR EGGS

Sooner or later you knew we would have to eat them, didn't you? Why else would we have prepared them so carefully, dressed them so appealingly?

Look how cute that one looks all dressed up in gold lamé and silk, with its ten-gallon hat, xxxx beaver, setting on its head. Hiya Pardner! No time for compassion now, though. Gulp! And a happy Easter to you, too.

Tag-Sale Terror

My late mother had a tag sale last weekend, an experience I shall not soon forget, though I will certainly try.

The reason I say "my late mother" is that Saturday afternoon, either from terror or panic, or both, my mother passed out on the living-room floor and was promptly purchased by a little old lady with a wheelbarrow for $165 and carted off. What really infuriated me was that I love my mother deeply and hated to let her go fully $85 under the listed tag price. The little old lady sure made some buy.

In any event, for those of you who have not yet had the good fortune to participate in a genuine tag sale, or better yet, had one of your very own, I thought I'd describe the phenomenon to you and deliver a few pointers on how to survive.

TUESDAY–THURSDAY

The five suburban housewives from Wicky Wacky Brica Bracky who, when they are not running tag sales, are gunrunners for Fidel Castro set up camp in your house and proceed to estimate the value of your possessions. To do this they rely on a time-tested formula. You reluctantly tell them what the lowest price you will take for an item is, then divide by ten, subtract twice the actual value, halve that, and mark it accordingly, leaving room for serious negotiation. You must secretly re-mark the items upward when they are not looking.

FRIDAY—DAY OF SALE

7 A.M.

The prospective buyers (vultures would be a better word) queue up outside your front door, peering in windows, eating their breakfast, and perching on telephone wires. From time to time they give evidence of being restless by pounding on your bell. Throw them some fish, the sale doesn't officially begin until 9 A.M. Also keep a cattle prod around in case one breaks ranks.

9 A.M.

Open the door with a smile, then quickly leap out of the way lest you get trampled by the friendly crowd. If you have some tranquilizers handy, take just enough to sedate a herd of wild elephants.

9:01—5:30

The ensuing scene can best be likened to that of a stray animal in a river being attacked by a school of piranhas. Cope by locking yourself in the bathroom or dressing as a kumquat.

FRIDAY NIGHT

Do yoga. Spend the night reciting your mantra, "Why? why? why?"

SATURDAY

The piranhas return to strip the carcass clean. You are told there is a bid on the antique lowboy of $1.75, slightly below the $2,000 tag price. "Take it," you are advised, or risk being stuck, a fate clearly worse than death.

Someone tactfully inquires as to whether the sweater you are wearing is for sale. Just as tactfully you call into question the legitimacy of his birth and are restrained by two strong arms from Wicky Wacky.

By 5 P.M. there is little left save the floor and walls of the house and one desperado is working feverishly with a crowbar on these. Out the living-room window the sun is beginning to set and you strongly suspect it is trying to tell you something. It is time to become philosophical and take comfort from the wisdom of the sages. "C'est la vie," "Que sera, sera," and "He who laughs last laughs best." If you don't know any good wisdom, 100 proof bourbon will serve.

SATURDAY EVENING

The crew from Wicky Wacky Brica Bracky, who have been working like Trojans to get you 1 percent of what your belongings are worth (when they weren't having coffee), depart in an armored Brinks truck. They must prepare for tomorrow's sale around the corner.

SUNDAY

You take a parting look at what was once your home and then head for the sanitarium where you have wisely reserved a suite under your new name, Job.

En route you see a sign posted on a tree. It reads TAG SALE and points to a house where lines of cars are already beginning to form. You pause momentarily and say a silent prayer for the occupants, then run like hell.

A Volley
of Words

Despite the richness of the American language, there are occasional gaps, places where, for lack of an exact word, several must do. Though new words are constantly filtering into the language from diverse sources, few persons, to my knowledge, are intentionally and professionally creating them.

I am one of those persons and am considered in the trade, along with Ambrose Bierce, a master lexicraftologist. Unfortunately, poor Ambrose passed away some years ago, so I am alone in the field.

Many of the examples included here are culled from my early writings, which may account for their relative unfamiliarity.

My interest in lexicraftology derives chiefly from an ancestor, twenty generations removed, who first created the article "the." Some say he would be justly proud of me, were he still around, and that I am his "bois de dard," but they may be exaggerating my accomplishments. In any event, it is my hope that the reader will not only be illumined by the words here presented, but will feel obliged to adapt them to his own style and needs.

abdolatry, n.	fashionable irreverence
andelian, adj.	capable of negotiating high places
anphelopsis, n.	total ennui, disinterest
aristotropic, adj.	tending toward things aristocratic, much in the way a heliotropic plant tends toward the sun
arvine, adj.	dweller of the fields, such as the field mouse, *ex.* The *arvine* creature ran hither and yon.
autotoll, n.	toll bridge—exact-change line
befrought, adj.	to be overwhelmed mentally
blastworker, n.	one who works with explosives, i.e., nitro, dynamite, TNT, etc.
bois de bard, n.	Fr., wood of the dart—open to interpretation
bombane, v.	to hurl invective and contumely
carboil, n.	the solidified oil and grease bubbles which adorn the underside of a car
casselanaire, n., v.	pipe dream, fanciful creation
cerenibrium, n.	narcotized tranquillity

copulescence, n.	the healthy afterglow which attends successful intercourse
cuptone, n.	the sound made by cupping the hand over the ear
darkling, n.	one who is depressed or chronically melancholy
delint, v.	to remove lint
devile, v.	to think of as a devil
dipsonate, v.	to force alcoholic beverages on another person
dort, n.	small object of scorn and derision
drisme, adj.	weather which is both dreary and wet (rainy)
eggplantine, adj.	color or shape of an eggplant
enfemic, adj.	peculiar to women
ergroid, adj.	crude, devoid of politesse
exarbiter, n.	sophist
exorcyst, n.	one who engages in elaborate and arcane ritual for the purpose of removing sebaceous carbuncles
fandible, n.	dance move in which fan dancer flourishes fan
fasole, v.	to physically calm or restrain
flamanous, adj.	provocative, inflammatory
floit, v.	to flaunt sexually
forgue, v.	to gouge or spear with a poisonous instrument
gnord, n.	large chasm
gonf, n.	thief, from the Yiddish goniff

gorcon, n. — mythological animal with head of a frog and body of a duck

gorcozoid, adj. — of or pertaining to a gorcon

graphoon, n. — verbal cartoon, vignette, *see* litoon

harveylike, adj. — similar in appearance to Harvey

hopsole, n. — the rear or ventral fin of the gefilte fish

horndite, n. — esoteric sexual allusion, *ex.* The article was replete with obscurantist references and *horndite*.

hyponious, adj. — given to flights of imagination, fanciful

iiant, n. — giant pygmy native to the leeward Antilles. Because of its unusual size, the iiant is usually indistinguishable from anyone else.

insorcible, adj. — magically intractable

iracent, adj. — glowing with anger

janoril, n. — miniature sunflower seldom found in either hemisphere. It was discovered in 1877 by the German botanist Gottfried von Duberstuüng. In 1908, the drug misaril was synthesized from the stamen of the janoril flower and was used to treat rampant pinheadism.

janoril, n. (cont.)
Due to the rarity of the janoril plant, production of misaril was terminated in 1909, thus explaining the continued virulence of R.P.

josan, n.
the fourth primary color, the others being red, yellow, and blue

kapula, n.
in grammar, the reticulated participle, when juxtaposed transitively with a split infinitive

kikidoori, n.
a pearl-like growth occasionally uncovered during root-canal surgery

kisantel, n.
coquette

klonce, n.
crotch

lapant, n.
lasciviously hungry individual; sufferer from satyriasis or nymphomania

lasarene, n.
cold, one who is hyperborean in temperament

licid, adj.
opposite of viscous, thin quality of a liquid

litoon, n.
humorous vignette, *see* graphoon

lolodacity, n.
campaign strategy peculiar to many politicians in which they hit far below the belt

malactive, adj.
evilly busy, up-to-no-good, *ex.* the *malactive* Mrs. Mintz

mondeveneer, n.
a false worldliness, *ex.* The count assumed a *mondeveneer.*

monodigital, adj.
the action of one finger, *ex.* He was a *monodigital* typist.

myhx, n.
the premature blond streak often seen running through the hair of young women

mystoplicsis, n.
the action of the eyes following the misdirection of a prestidigitator

nacilious, adj.
of or pertaining to an adult who uses baby talk

nausilatory, adj.
action in which one concedes, but continues to feel nauseous

nocturanian, n.
1. that genus of raccoon which is both nocturnal and garbage eating; 2. any creature of the evening

nonono, adv.
extreme form of the negative, no!

nudements, n.
rules of pornography

obstilibut, n.
that end of a syringe which points away from the face

orealaby, n.
a syllabus or compendium of humorous writing

osantine, adj.
of or pertaining to oozing

ossis, n.
the contents of a black hole

pantonomic, adj.
pertaining to the act of patting a friend on the derriere, *ex.* football players

phallander, n.
a rare species of salamander, characterized, as is the fiddler crab, by one outsized member

popsynopsis, n.
exceedingly short summary

porcule, adj.
round of face

psintoid, adj.
pertaining to tongue twisters

quatressential, adj.
not quite quintessential

quorbus, n.
archaic, a carnivorous plant once found in parts of New Guinea and believed to consume virgins. When brought to civilization, it rapidly became extinct. No follow-up study was ever done.

rackle, v.
to grate on one's nerves

ramiform, adj.
while Webster defines ramiform as a branch or resembling a branch, few people are aware that Ramiform I was also the pharaoh of Egypt from 451–450 B.C. He is not much discussed in history books, having ended his life after one year as pharaoh by butting his head into a pyramid, causing great embarrassment to the Egyptians of the time. Thus, while his name has been

ramiform, adj. (cont.)	carefully deleted from most histories, the word ramiform has come to mean the manner of ending one's life by butting one's head. There was no Ramiform II.
recantle, v.	to relate ad tedium
resofincular, adj.	resembling a wire hanger
rhapsorinth, n.	the ten tasks which must be performed before becoming a member of The Ellosinian Mysts
salimony, n.	state of embarrassed poverty
schreck, n.	screaming wife
simplectic, adj.	so simple as to be absurd
stargle, v.	to choke, making gurgling noises
sucrest, v.	to take forcibly
superbrite, n.	individual whose I.Q. exceeds 180
tandrome, n.	portable elephant house
tanteloupe, n.	sorcerer's cap
testiferous, adj.	uppity, agitated
trigatory, adj.	an arrangement of three, *ex.* He entered into a *trigatory* relationship.
ulanimity, n.	complete satiety, contentment
umdrill, n.	state of bewilderment, darkness
vistant, adj.	within visible range
vixative, adj.	pertaining to undisciplined study habits

wampoles, n.

pl., the vertical sticks used in constructing a teepee or tent

wendigant, adj.

wayward, stray

wystemious, adj.

given to circumlocution and double-talk

xenoralia, n.

foreign idioms and expressions

yost, v.

to lift an extremely heavy object, to strain

yukatory, adj.

relating to things vulgar or disgusting

zonoobia, n.

fantasy state, deep reverie

Magic on My Mind

*A*s a magician I am not supposed to reveal my tricks, but neither was I supposed to turn in my grandmother, even though it was common knowledge she was a hit man for the Mafia. My doctor says I have mixed ethical preferences and that I should stay out of Brooklyn. My doctor is married to my grandmother and says she just did what she had to. She says she has to get me.

I think everyone should be able to do tricks, not just amateur magicians and the professionals on the East Side. Have you ever wondered how the magician is able to pull Harriet the rabbit out of his hat, and why Harriet has a funny look on her face? Or thrilled to the escape artist who locks himself into a trunk, impossibly secured, only to reappear moments later as a tournament Ping-Pong ball? These, my friends, are secrets meant to be shared with others, not hoarded selfishly like Velveeta cheese.

Recently the magician Flasho, whose name derives from his avocation, revealed some of his secrets to the public. Unfortunately, he was picked up by a local patrolman who already knew his secrets, and he barely managed a suspended sentence. Such is the delicate nature of the subject at hand. Nevertheless, in the interest of all mankind, and twenty bucks, I shall here reveal some of the profound and most guarded secrets of my craft.

Misdirection

Certainly one of the magician's major tools is misdirection. He uses it frequently to distract the spectator while he palms a small assistant or eggplant. Anything which focuses the spectator's eye elsewhere will serve, i.e., a death in the room or pneumatic jackhammer. Without misdirection the magician is like a politician who speaks from the heart.

Patter

Patter is to magic what music is to singing; it augments the magician's performance and helps keep him awake. Sometimes it takes the form of a story in which a silk or an egg is the hero. This type of sophisticated patter demands something of the audience and is most effective when playing before a crate of oranges or dentists. Patter may also be used with little feet.

Sleight of Hand

There is no truth to the old chestnut "the hand is quicker than the eye." In any race between an eye and a hand, the eye will win every time. In fact, recently an eye running against a strong field of assorted anatomical parts outdistanced all but a particularly swift sinus.

Sleight of hand is actually used under cover of misdirection, such as when the magician shouts "Look over there" and steals your wallet. If magicians were paid an adequate wage, they would not have to use sleight of hand.

Sawing a Woman in Half

Sawing a woman in half is the goal of many aspiring magicians and henpecked husbands. It is not as difficult as it looks, unless you also want to restore the woman to her whole self.

For this trick you will require a wooden box and a willing woman. The former is easily obtained from any reputable funeral parlor and the latter from a singles bar. Place the woman in the box (preferably with manacles) so that her head sticks out one end and her feet the other. Then proceed to saw.

On performing this illusion the first few times it is advisable to wear cotton in the ears and a machine-washable apron. Also a good lawyer wouldn't hurt. After you get the hang of it you can dispense with the cotton.

Levitation

Effect: The assistant lies down on a divan and is covered with a large spangled cloth. At the magician's command the assistant appears to rise several feet into the air.

Execution: This feat is easily accomplished when at the proper moment the magician releases a tarantula into the assistant's drawers.

As you can see, magic is an art like basting chickens, or evading taxes. It must be practiced until perfect. Not long ago a young conjurer foolishly changed himself into a frankfurter at Yankee Stadium and was never heard from again. Just as in other businesses, magic is dog eat dog.

The Book
of Lisps

As you can see from having tried to recite the title of
this piece ten times in a row, fast, and failed, you have
a lisp. So let's address the problem squarely, call a lisp a
lisp, and see what we can do about it.

First off, what is a lisp?

A lisp is any speech impediment or deviation from the
normal speech pattern in which you spit all over people
and drench them head to foot. Even if you are drinking
orange soda just as somebody tells a joke and you explode
the soda in all directions at once, it counts as a lisp. Or
it can be when you try to say "Is that so?" and instead
say, "Ith that tho?"; and although you are a shot-putter
in the Soviet Army wearing a green beret and a tattoo of
a snake chewing a tank across your chest, people ask
you questions about *Swan Lake* and silk pongee and bone

china. Or it can be that you constantly punctuate your speech with "you know" when you don't know, and that is definitely a lisp. Or you say "nu-kyoo-ler," for "noo-kleer," that is a lisp. Or you say "R" for "L," as in "rolly pop"—all Chinese have lisps, 900,000,000 of them. My book is a big hit in Peking. Or if you include in your discourse references to "Mac" or "Chief," you have a lisp. "Hey Mac, pull it over." All police have lisps, especially state troopers and parkway fuzz, though the latter sometimes try to compensate for their speech disfluency by substituting "Buddy" for "Chief" or "Mac." Or you may be into vitamin E and free radicals. All health-food buffs and nutrinos have lisps. Are you in analysis, or therapy? You have a big lisp, God help you Buddy!

Ultimately, even those of us who seemingly do not have a lisp trip up on tongue twisters when we are asked, for example, to say "Thithm Squetchl Strithmdum Plicth" rapidly in public, or "Blig, Blag, Blug, Bluth, Bloth," which is trotted out more than you might expect these days, especially in the heat of argument. That last one always manages to catch me off guard, though you probably have more success than I with it. "Blig, Blag, Blumth, Blotch"—Blech!

BAD LISPS
Rhinolisp

One of the worst lisps (fortunately it only afflicts a very few persons) is Rhinolisp in which the individual afflicted is seized with an uncontrollable urge to go "Rhino" right in the middle of a sentence or whatever else he or she is doing.

Example: "As we were saying a moment ago 'Rhino' in reference to the balance-of-payments schedule." Or, "Oh! Hi there Mary, 'Rhino.' Good to see you."

If 'Rhino' is accompanied by the sprouting of a horn on the bridge of the nose, help should be sought immediately.

No-Lisp

No-lisp is a terrible condition in which the lisper effects no speech impediment whatsoever, no rolled L's, no tied tongue, no stammer, tics, or spray. It is positively awful. Most people in the presence of a no-lisp sufferer become so intimidated and uneasy that they turn on their heels and flee within moments of identifying the affliction.

Fortunately, very few people have no-lisp.

Apocalisp

Apocalisp is so severe and disabling that it is almost obscene. In fact, if you encounter a person with apocalisp, it is probably better not to look or listen. Just close your eyes and cover your ears and wait until the poor soul goes on its way. For the stout of heart this is what occurs. The lisper suddenly begins to metamorphose much the way a werewolf does, only into the letter "S," bent and crooked. From his lips is emitted a hideous, sibilant "sssssssss" "sssssssss" sound, like the song of a serpent or the slough of the wind. The lisper remains thus transmogrified until the seizure has passed, when slowly he returns to normal. Some people who have witnessed an apocalisp firsthand say it is the most terrifying experience they have ever had, a human being transformed into a letter right before their eyes. They don't even like to talk about it.

If you are a lisper and have a mild to moderate problem, it would probably be wise to seek professional help. There are exercises that have been developed, mouth-checks, and other techniques that can turn a lisper into a clear-speaking member of the community. You have but to avail yourself of these services.

If, however, you show premorbid signs of either Rhin-olisp or Apocalisp, you have serious trouble. Run, don't walk to your nearest speech emergency clinic and throw yourself inside, schnell. Pray that it is not too late.

Oh no! Not me, not now, "sssssssss," I can't believe it, "sssssssss" "sssssssssss" "sssssssssss."

Close Encounters of the Fourth Kind

*F*or centuries relationships between humans and trees were thought by the general public to be unhealthy, if not outright depraved. Lovers so inclined were forced to maintain clandestine relationships and to seek each other out in the forest at night. Anyone caught enjoying the favors of an attractive weeping willow in seventeenth-century France, for example, was beheaded on the spot, and even in our own time, homo-herbo love is considered a mark of disgrace except among Mormons who date whole forest preserves and state parks when no one's looking.

Actually, premarital intercourse between an individual and a tree, as long as it is performed by two consenting adults (no youngsters under eighteen or saplings) who do not subject the other to the danger of pregnancy or venereal disease such as syphilis, gonorrhea, or scale, or use any degree of force or coercion, is an entirely moral and ethical act.

Likewise, petting between humans and trees is entirely moral, though oral root contact will have to be considered separately.

But ethical questions aside, there are still further obstacles to be overcome if one is to successfully love a tree.

For one thing, the sheer size of some trees makes physical intimacy next to impossible. The tragic story of the frail wine-maiden and the giant sequoia serves to illustrate this point. A wine-maiden fell in love with a giant sequoia while tending her vines one afternoon and resolved to give herself to the tree that night. When she was found the next morning hanging by her nose from a nearby mountain, her family chopped the tree down and ground it into sawdust. They never even noticed the ear-to-ear smile of contentment that ringed the wine-maiden's face. Till the day she died the wine-maiden never forgot the sequoia tree and wore her splinters with pride.

Foliage, too, can prove a problem for potential lovers. Legion are the tales of pine and spruce fanciers who have ended their affairs only because they could no longer bear being punctured by a thousand needles during sex. Or the oak and sumac wooers who came down the next morning with severe rash over the entire surface of their bodies.

But as with other forms of hazardous love, the differences dividing the two life forms at times serves rather as a spur than as a stop. In some cases it even inflames the passions.

Who has not watched a crazy fool leap headlong into the branches of his waiting lover only to be dashed to death moments later when the wind shakes him sixty feet to the ground? Animal-vegetable love is not for the faint of heart.

If you choose to pursue a love relationship with a tree, and I am not advising that you do so, there are certain factors that should be taken into account:

1. Trees are stationary. You cannot take them to a drive-in movie, or even the opera. What's worse, they do it right out in the open.
2. Trees do not talk, which can be either an asset or a detriment depending on where you're coming from.
3. Deciduous trees shed their leaves in the fall and winter. It is the equivalent of looking at a wife in pin curls from October to April.
4. Trees, especially the larger ones, will probably outlive you by several hundred or a thousand years. Thus you must be prepared for your tree to become involved with other lovers or marry several times after you are gone.
5. Unless you adopt, children are out of the question. Fruit, however, is a possibility.
6. If you have never had Dutch elm disease before, get shots before dating an elm.

In the final analysis, having an encounter with a tree, whether sexual or strictly on the up and up, can be both a unique and a rewarding experience. Just don't tell your friends about it.

The Sushi of Life

*T*here is little question that sushi, the extraordinary Japanese delicacy which wraps raw things in vinegared rice and crisp vitamin-rich nori seaweed, has caught on here in the West. Witness the proliferation of new life-sushi delights which have evolved.

BLUSUTO

Blusuto or blue suit sushi is found only in the best department stores and specialty shops and made from the freshest cloth. It is considered particularly good. To prepare blusuto the sushi chef first removes the buttons from the front of the jacket and the cuffs, then carefully makes two 18-inch cuts in the belly of the trousers and lifts out the zipper. This done, the suit is folded carefully into a square and placed on top of the rice and wrapped with seaweed. As a rule, blusuto is served with wasabi root and sliced ginger. Caution: Unless blusuto has been fileted, one should watch out for pins.

PORSCHE

Good Porsche is a treat for the eye as well as the palate. One of the softest of the motored sushis, it is expensive and sleek and must be experienced fresh off the assembly line, never secondhand or used. Porsche is usually served alone and unadorned, though one variety, racer-Porsche, is frequently garnished with small quantities of lubricating oil and antifreeze. Porsche are at their best between February and September when the highways are dry and light.

COKUBU SUSHI

Cokubu sushi, or coke, as it is more commonly referred to, is a potent form of maki sushi found only in certain select sushi parlors on the Upper East Side and backstage. Imported from the gold coast of Florida at night, cokubu sushi is rolled in seaweed and stuffed up the nose, followed by a dab of wasabi and ginger. If the coke doesn't blow your mind and set you afire, the wasabi sure as hell will. In Japan, cokubu sushi is known as dragon dust and makes the Japanese feel taller.

Hoho

Hoho, or laughing sushi, so called because of the horns and feathers which tickle on the way down, is one of the best loved and most widely experimented with forms of sushi. Napoleon had just eaten hoho before he crossed the Alps into Bavaria. Howard of Rome was an aficionado of hoho, as were the Duke and Duchess of Ink and Franz Klopf. Try hoho, it will tickle you—or at least itch.

Tele Maki

Tele maki is the communicating person's sushi. Instead of seaweed, the small transistors, chips, and diodes are rolled together in electrical tape and plugged into the nearest socket where, through the miracle of modern science, the eater is able to make long-distance calls to Japan. Should the eater wish to place calls to anyplace else in the world, however, he would be better off using a phone. For what it's worth, tele maki has been the sushi of choice with Japanese-American employees of AT&T for over twenty years now. Hello, can you hear me? Honda, Honda, help help me Honda.

Sushi Sundae

Made from tri-flavor ice cream, bean curd, octopus, and pickle, and surrounded by nuts, fruit, marshmallow, and hot-fudge sauce before being wrapped in rice and seaweed, sushi sundae is truly a gourmet fantasy. Served on a glass tray with a dollop of whipped wasabi and a maraschino cherry to add tang, sushi sundae is Nippon's gift to the Occident. Sweet sushi sundae, ummmh, aahhhhh!

Squimuro

Not much used in this country, squimuro or sushi nightmare is somewhat of a surprise to most diners untutored in the Japanese cuisinary arts. Suddenly you are grabbed by the sushi chef, perhaps with help from two other chefs if you kick and fuss, and packed head-to-toe in vinegared rice and wasabi. Next you are rolled in a six-foot blanket of nori seaweed, garnished with four or five pounds of ginger, maybe a bushel of onions, and fed to a giant lobster moving ponderously in the other room. Squimuro is the ultimate sushi experience, not to be missed. Save it for last, and, oh yes . . . Sayonara.

Fundamental Principles of Hysteria

*T*wice before in this century, great pioneers in the field of human funny business have shocked, informed, and transformed our world. In 1909, Harvey Ricknilster set forth the then revolutionary hypothesis that laughter does not originate in the belly as had been previously thought, but in the throat, exiting through the mouth. Forty years later, Wollenpoof and Droll actually caught a laugh trying to escape through the nose of a thirty-five-year-old New Jersey woman who had been tickled in a laboratory for over seventeen hours. They published their results in the now famous *Fundamental Principles of Hysteria* and kept the laugh alive for more than fifteen years by repeating a corny but effective Henny Youngman joke in its presence ten to twenty times a day. Their work has significantly shaped our attitudes about human laughter, influenced our behavior, and changed our lives in many ways; not the least effect being that mature people no longer shake their bellies like bowls full of jelly when they laugh, but give out full-bodied, throaty howls and peals when amused.

Now Wollenpoof and Droll have actually found and proved the existence of a second seat of interior convulsion, aptly named "The Giggle Spot," or G spot. When stimulated directly, the G spot begins to harden and vibrate, faster and faster, producing the characteristic snorts and titters which are so physiologically and psychologically distinct from coarse adult laughter. The G spot is a bean-shaped area within the anterior wall of the throat located midway between the fauces and the pharynx, facing the esophagus and abutting the laryngeal-tracheal highway. Without question it is the organ responsible for the silly, spasmodic gasps and whimpers that afflict many of us when we break up slowly and uncontrollably at the most inappropriate and unforgivable times and places.

"Daphne and I had been invited personally by Mr. Winston Figbottom to attend the DeGarpis lecture at the Institute. Scholars from all around the world had gathered this evening to hear the distinguished speaker deliver an important account of the new work he and his team had been doing. You could hear a pin drop. Then, as the speaker approached the rostrum, Daphne suddenly began to wrinkle up her nose as if she was going to sneeze. Then her features began to distort as at first she emitted only a single shrill rasp. I was attentive but not alarmed. Then slowly, crescendolike, she began to, to . . . there is no other way to adequately describe it, she began to giggle in a most unladylike and undignified fashion. Unable to calm her down by stuffing my handkerchief in her mouth, I proceeded to grab her neck and shake her, pressing with all my might on her cartoid arteries in the hope that I could stop her hysteria. Presently we were both escorted by ushers to the back of the hall and ejected forcibly in a most embarrassing manner. Obviously something had tickled Daphne in a new and alien way. In the past she had always been able to control her laughter at lectures. This time was different."

"Dorothy was a young mother seriously afflicted with atrabilia who had never been able to laugh or even chuckle. One day at breakfast a mote of dust or toast crumb went down the wrong pipe and set off such a flurry of inarticulate noises and sounds as to frighten her husband, who rushed her off to the emergency room of their local hospital. At the hospital the young intern in attendance identified the noises as unexpressed laughter or giggling that had probably been bottled up inside Dorothy for the better part of her life. He suggested her husband take her to the zoo where the hyenas could watch her."

The G-spot discovery and phenomenon lends credence to what many people have been feeling for a long time: that there are two different kinds of ha, ha-ing. It also synthesizes the theories of earlier researchers.

Another of Wallenpoof and Droll's extraordinary findings is that giggling is contagious, if not infectious. It is transmitted on the air through the sputa that is ejaculated during a fit of hysterics. While attacks of giggles are spontaneous and intermittent, they are apparently, like herpes, incurable. Sorry!

Space Chat

Arecibo, Puerto Rico

Recent advances in radio telescopy have made possible the first communication between our world and an intelligent life form from another part of the galaxy. This historic event has been duly recorded, and I feel fortunate to have received an unexpurgated transcript of the exchange from my friend Dr. De Long Sigmoid, who has translated it into language we can all understand.

The dialogue which follows is between Professor Sigmoid and the extraterrestrial creature who for personal reasons refers to himself as X3.

Sig: Hello!
X3: What?
Sig: Hello!

X3: What?

Sig: What?

X3: Hello?

Sig: Hello!

X3: Yes, who is this?

Sig: What?

X3: I said who is this?

Sig: This is Professor DeLong Sigmoid speaking to you from a radio telescope in Arecibo, Puerto Rico.

X3: Where?

Sig: Arecibo, Puerto Rico.

X3: Arecibo, Puerto Rico?

Sig: Yes, Arecibo, Puerto Rico.

X3: Can you speak louder?

Sig: Yes, who are you?

X3: Why do you want to know?

Sig: It is of historical importance.

X3: Are you taping this conversation?

Sig: Yes.

X3: Let's say I'm X3.

Sig: Where are you from?

X3: I am from Gool in the Galaxy Hex, but I am not Goolian.

Sig: You are not Goolian?

X3: Do I sound Goolian?

Sig: What are you then?

X3: My mother was a Bell, so I live on Gool but am a Bell.

Sig: You are a Bell correct?

X3: What is a Bellcorrect?

Sig: I mean you consider yourself a Bell.

X3: I am a Bell.

Sig: Alright, you are a Bell.

X3: I'm not sure I like your tone.

Sig: Please, X3, surely you understand the importance of this communication.

X3: I think you do not believe I am a bell.

Sig: I believe you are a Bell.

X3: You better believe it.

Sig: Can you describe the character of your civilization?

X3: If I'm not a Bell, then who is?

Sig: X3, your civilization, can you describe it?

X3: It's not enough these days to be a Bell, you have to convince people, ach!

Sig: Look, I apologize for in any way offending you. It was not my intention.

X3: If you only knew the abuse we Bells have to put up with!

Sig: I'm truly sorry

X3: From another galaxy no less.

Sig: X3?

X3: From an Areciban or whatever the Gool you are.

Sig: What source of power are you using to transmit?

X3: Holy helix, what gall! What impertinence! This across a thousand light-years.

Sig: X3, the fact that we have established contact is a monumental achievement, it will go down . . .

X3: A Gool am I, you ridiculous creature.

Sig: Forgive me X3, certainly this is a misunderstanding, my people . . .

X3: I have a good mind to terminate this conversation.

Sig: For God's sake, in the interest of intelligent life everywhere, don't terminate our communication.

X3: Who am I?

Sig: You are a Bell, a beautiful Bell.

X3: I knew it, I am not beautiful. I do not have to reach through the universe to be insulted.

Sig: I did not know.

X3: You did not know?

Sig: Please believe me.

X3: You are forgiven; what do you want?

Sig: What are you like? Can you depict yourself, your form, your essence?

X3: I am relatively small, more round than ovoid, wafer on the bottom, marshmallow on top, and covered with chocolate excrescence.

Sig: Like a Mallomar?

X3: You know Mallomars?

Sig: My children eat them all the time.

X3: They eat Mallomars? My God! That would explain probe I and probe II. Mallomars are the principal inhabitants of Gool.

Sig: X3, we are a civilized people.

X3: Hardly.

Sig: We are a highly technological society.

X3: Have you the technology to traverse space, say to Gool?

Sig: We do not as yet possess technological means of that sophistication.

X3: Phew!

Sig: Obviously your society is highly civilized, if not in advance of our own.

X3: Obviously. Mallomars are highly civilized and intelligent beings, especially Bell Mallomars.

Sig: Bell Mallomars?

X3: Bell Mallomars such as myself have small bell configurations on their bodies exactly in the center. Ordinary Mallomars are smooth on top.

Sig: Do you live in cities?

X3: We are not mobile as you Arecibans, we are instead able to fluoresce.

Sig: Fluoresce?

X3: I'd rather not go into it. I suspect fluorescent Mallomars are beyond your ken.

Sig: How do you reproduce?

X3: I beg your pardon!

Sig: Reproduce, have offspring.

X3:   I will not discuss that sort of thing over a radio telescope.

Sig: X3, I am a scientist.

X3:   You remind me of those voyeurs on Venus. Why don't you ask them how we reproduce?

Sig: You mean there are intelligent beings on Venus?

X3:   I didn't say intelligent.

Sig: We assumed Venus to be uninhabitable.

X3:   Give them a buzz, you would have much in common.

Sig: Are there any other inhabited planets within our solar system?

X3:   I hear there are some strange creatures on Earth.

Sig: I am from Earth.

X3:   I thought you were from Arecibo?

Sig: Arecibo is on Earth.

X3:   Do you Arecibans read Grogle?

Sig: Who?

X3:   Grogle!

Sig: I'm sorry I can't hear you.

X3:   Grogle!

Sig: Gargle? Godl . . .

X3:   Listen, it's been good chatting with you.

Sig: But . . .

X3:   *Click*

The Shape of Things to Come

*B*ecause of my reputation as a life-scape architect specializing in bio-design (I studied with Crick, Watson, and I. M. Pei), I have been hired by God Himself to evaluate the grand scheme of things and find ways of improving it. His Omnipotence is not happy with the human condition as it now stands and wants a new plan by Friday. He is especially unhappy about birth and death because shades have told him that death is no way to repay seventy or eighty years of devotion and service. A gold watch perhaps, a plaque signed by friends and relatives, but not death. Death is so, how do you say in English, "yucky." And I agree. Thus I have set about to redesign the order of life as we know it and make it more palatable to all concerned while still allowing "you know who" to summon us to the great beyond when He wants us.

A major part of my eschatological plan has to do with beginnings and endings and calls for a dramatic reversal of the two. Instead of being born first and developing slowly through infancy, childhood, and maturity only to decline in old age, we would begin in death and move rapidly through senescence, ill health, and adulthood, growing stronger and healthier every day. In this way we'd get the misery and sickness out of the way quick and be able to enjoy the rest of our lives without fear of death. Heart disease and cancer would happen early; we'd go out fit as fiddles.

"Oh! Hi Mary, how's the new baby?"

"Not so well, Florabelle, he's recuperating from triple bypass surgery, but thank God, the doctors say he'll be up and around in a few weeks."

"And your little girl?"

"Jennifer is wonderful, thanks, threw her cane away last week, and her hair is starting to turn brown."

Growing older, we'd grow healthier and happier. At the end we would pass through St. Peter's gate like so many Olympic athletes at a decathlon.

"God, I feel great."

"That's good son, come with me."

Or:

"Wow, I feel like a million bucks!"

Poof!

"Did you see that? One minute this handsome, healthy, terrific-looking guy is standing there, and the next minute he vanishes into thin air."

"Yeah, it must have been his time. But did you see that smile on his face? Yup."

"I can't wait till it's my turn."

"Me neither."

Part two of my plan sets forth some minor improvements in the human anatomy which should markedly enhance the quality of life for generations to come.

THE EXTRA DISPOSABLE STOMACH

The extra disposable stomach is a bifurcated affair which allows the individual to eat both for nutrition and for fun.

Consider your average fatty. He consumes enough food to ensure sound nutrition, but then goes on, and on, and on like a vacuum cleaner. With the extra disposable stomach our little blubberball could eat as much as he wished. Having finished a proper meal, he simply switches to stomach B and stuffs it with figs, dates, cake, ice cream, and candy, then unhooks it and throws it away. He attaches a new stomach and starts all over again. He would not gain weight, he would not feel guilty. Sound good? It's in the works.

THE SELF-CLEANING NOSE

The self-cleaning nose looks like any other, it is just more efficient, automatic. Good-by tissues. Good-by hankies. It will have a minor impact on the nasal decongestant industry until it is discovered that Dristan can be used in clogged sinks and sewers with equal effectiveness. A shift in marketing direction will more than compensate.

TAPE CASSETTE PLAYER

Certain individuals, along with the onset of puberty, will develop a crease in the chest into which a tape cassette may be inserted. Volume and tuning controls will appear at the base of the neck shortly thereafter. Besides providing these individuals with an internal musical system, so necessary these days, the tape cassette player will make them popular with their peers.

"Hey Jack, shove another tape into Harvey, will you?"

"Thanks man."

Harvey will never be alone again.

FOOT WHEELS

As with the tape cassette player, only certain individuals will develop foot wheels. These will first appear as small protuberances on the soles of the feet around the age of eight or nine. By twelve the wheels will be fully formed and able to turn. They are retractable and ever-bearing. It is my hope that they will revolutionize the short-trip industry.

Finally, and to my way of thinking the most important part of my plan, man needs an outlet. This is critical, so I have provided him with one where the left elbow used to be—220 volts, alternating current.

I am optimistic that my plan will be accepted by the powers that be and that God will back me all the way. He has indicated that He will. I certainly hope so, for your sake.

The Case
of Child C

Studies of children with I.Q.s in the gifted range are
very rare, though not so rare as studies of pregnant tent
caterpillars with athlete's foot. Nevertheless, when they
occur, these studies often shed light on important questions concerning the nature of intelligence and why certain children are better able to do *The New York Times*
crossword puzzle than other children.

It is commonplace to hear of boys and girls with extremely high I.Q.s, in fact most of us do, from new parents. Unfortunately, the preponderance of these
exceedingly bright youngsters only remains bright until
tested by a bona fide psychologist, whereupon their brains
fail them and they are labeled with some odious epithet
such as "normal" or "above average," the latter term being
particularly offensive for some reason.

Thus, when a genuine gifted child, with no strings attached, surfaces, it is cause for much jubilation among the scientific community. This is the case of Child C.

CHILD C

Child C is a boy, born June 5, 1946. He was brought to the writer's attention by the principal of Public School 646 in Manhattan, who thought it unusual that a youngster of three could make a palindrome out of the *Encyclopaedia Britannica.*

FAMILY BACKGROUND

Child C is descended in both lines from German Jews, which is odd as his parents are Mexican Catholics who think "Matzoh Brei" is a Japanese board game. They named him Child C to differentiate him from their other children, A, B, and D. Despite his awareness that he has two brothers and a sister, C insists that he is an only child. His siblings understand this little quirk and affectionately refer to him as "asshole."

PRESCHOOL HISTORY

Evidence of precocity is illustrated by the fact that C began to walk at the age of nine months. He also began to talk at nine months. Because these two events occurred at precisely the same time, his parents were unable to tell which was which, and to this day maintain that C walks too fast.

When he was four years old C went one day to a store with his father. While the latter was making his purchases, the child began to scan some books lying on a shelf. The shopkeeper noticed the boy looking attentively at the books and said as a joke, "Boy, if you can read me that book I will give it to you." Instantly C began to read fluently and carried the book away from the astonished merchant. With their ventriloquism act C and his father were able to build quite a good-sized library.

School Life

In school C's teachers recognized him as out of the ordinary but thought him queer and odd because of his strange habit of embalming fellow students. In spite of perfect work he was advanced only ten grades, which caused him to be unhappy. This resulted in the guidance office having him tested, whereupon it was revealed he had the mental level of a herd of elephants.

When he was nine years old the following conversation took place:

Q. Do you like to read?
A. Do you like to read?
Q. Would you like to go to college?
A. Would you like to go to college?

The answers to these questions show that C is keenly aware of his own abilities and also that he is a mimic. This trait has not endeared him to his peers, who on more than one occasion have tried to erase his head. In the school play, *Robinson Crusoe,* C gave a superior performance as the parrot.

CHARACTER

A few character flaws in C have been noted by his teachers. One teacher said, "He is somewhat mischievous." This impression appears to be based partly on the fact that he has detonated several nuclear devices in the washroom and partly on his need to rut with sporting equipment.

Nor does C take well to competition. Soon after he entered the special opportunity class for gifted children another boy equaled him in an assignment and put out his hand to C, saying cordially, "Let's shake." C had never had the experience of being equaled by a fellow pupil and was so surprised that he inadvertently poured 200 cubic centimeters of sulfuric acid into the boy's milk during lunch.

AFTERWARD

C was graduated from college summa cum laude having majored in foreign languages. At the time of his graduation he spoke fifty-six languages fluently, two of which were known. Soon after college he joined the army and served two years against his will as a military podiatrist. He was decorated twice, once for bravery and once by a drunk who mistook him for the Easter Bunny. Upon reentering civilian life C became a political activist and wrote numerous letters to the State Department protesting the cholesterol count, which he viewed as subversive. Depressed by the failure of his campaign, he unsuccessfully attempted to commit suicide by consuming two dozen eggs laced with red meat. This experience seemed to have an uplifting effect on his life, and he found steady work as an alcoholic on the Lower East Side.

It was during this period that C developed an insatiable craving for clean sheets and married Hester Cornstarch, first iron at the Consolidated Laundries. They have two children and a large dog whose bladder frequently runs amok.

POSTSCRIPT

The case of child C raises the question of whether an exceedingly gifted child such as child C can ever make a "normal" adjustment to society. From the evidence at hand the answer would appear to be "no way." However, C himself has suggested that he was a "normal" child and that it is everyone else who must strive for "normal" adjustment. He further suggests that our study is a "crock" and that we should leave him to his "bees," which he does not bother to explain. In compliance with his wishes, no follow-up studies are planned. I might add that in this writer's opinion, C was always a "pain."

TV Special

If all goes as planned, next Saturday's war between the United States and the Union Of Soviet Socialist Republics should prove the greatest single conflagration in martial history, eclipsing even "The Bam in Nam" for sheer pyrotechnics.

Bob Arum and Don King, promoters of the war, have assured both sides of enormous gains. The U.S.S.R. stands to retrieve umpteen zillion barrels of crude oil and all the grain it can eat; while the U.S., if it wins, will be in caviar and Stolchinaya till time immemorial.

Arum, who ended his feud with Don King long enough to co-promote the scheduled four-day war, predicted that the United States' share of closed-circuit television revenues, in addition to the $3 billion from the live gate sale to Switzerland, would at least equal what Nolan Ryan of the Houston Astros earned during the years 1978–1983.

Hitherto, the record take by any participant in a toe-to-toe slugfest was the $10 million Sugar Ray Leonard received for his bout with Roberto Duran in Montreal four years ago. But as a sporting event the upcoming inter-necine war has no historical antecedents. "The Super Bowl is peanuts compared to this one," said Arum, who fore-sees the closed-circuit and foreign TV revenues going beyond $300 billion. "I mean this is the real thing," he continued, "Armageddon," and then sank back in his chair as if to contemplate the biblical grandeur of it all.

In the Middle East where the war is likely to begin, preparations were under way yesterday and today to en-sure that cameramen and TV crews would be safe from fallout from the war itself. Analysts expect that the war will begin with conventional weapons and quickly esca-late to a nuclear confrontation, perhaps as early as Sun-day. The first shot should come around 10:30 P.M. New York time so that it can be seen clearly by impartial ob-servers, but could be delayed until 11:00 pending the results of promotional arrangements.

"World War III," as it is being ballyhooed by the media and press agents from both sides, can be seen on forty thousand closed-circuit TV sites in this hemisphere and ten thousand more in Asia and Africa; there will be no live home television or radio except for pay-TV in Colum-bus, Ohio, and some remote areas in the Ukraine. Most people, however, believe they will be able to see at least some of the war without TV.

The undefeated United States is the 7–5 betting favor-ite, perhaps a reflection more of its popularity among potential beneficiaries of foreign aid then of the relative strengths of the combatants.

Cap Weinberger, the U.S. coach, said today he expected the United States to try for a fast knockout but added that he could not reveal any top-secret strategies or plans that might tip "The Big Red Machine." The Joint Chiefs of Staff, who have been training the armed forces, said they were ready.

Herman Kahn, the United States strategist, said he had spent countless hours studying the U.S.S.R. through satellite tapes and reruns of *War and Peace*. "All countries have weaknesses," said Kahn, "and the U.S.S.R. is no exception. It was invaded by the Germans years ago and almost lost. Remember, we are holding China back on a leash. The U.S.S.R. has big juicy borders."

Kahn, who has also managed several lightweight South American countries, says, "If there's one country I understand, it's Russia. They're all bluff and bluster. My country will blow them away. You can make book on it."

The United States has not seemed right to America Watchers lately, including some who are picking it to win. Unemployment was up last quarter while inflation continued to erode the much-vaunted Reagan dollar. In general, the economy appeared sluggish, and the President, in a speech before The Academy of Motion Picture Sciences, admitted that there was too much fat in the military. "If Congress had approved all my cuts we would have been much trimmer," said the President. "But we'll be ready come next Saturday," he said smiling benevolently to reporters.

Staff members close to the President speculate that he may just have been trying to lower the odds.

As for the U.S.S.R., it has remained cool in the face of what many intelligence agents consider its sternest military test yet. In a prepared statement to TASS, the official Soviet news agency, Marshall Dumbkoff Zhukov, the Russian coach trying to play down hostilities between the countries, said, "The Soviet people's juggernaut will crush the capitalist aggressors like the stupid worms they are."

In any event it is common knowledge here in the West that the Soviet army numbers almost 4 million men and women, all of whom won gold medals in gymnastics at the last Olympics. This in itself would be cause for concern, but the Russians also are known to possess what some experts call "essential equivalence," a secret weapon of the most hideous proportions. One U.S. general, asked to comment on the Soviet secret weapon, said, "We had "essential equivalence" in Nam and it didn't mean diddly. 'Essential equivalence' is strictly media hype."

Here is how the two sides stack up in terms of strategic weaponry and manpower.

	U.S.	**U.S.S.R.**
Men under Arms	1.5 million	3.6 million
ICBMs: Nuked	1,054	1,398
Sub—Missiles	656	950
M-80s	50,000	60,000
Cherry Bombs	35,000	20,000

As far as the outcome, the experts are divided. Some see the U.S. winning, because of superior technology and aim. Others point to the U.S.S.R.'s ability to deliver larger payloads.

One wag predicted the war would be cosmological; big bang—black hole. As we go to press it's 7–5, pick 'em.

An Official Register of Important Names

*C*aution: Should even one of the following names coincide with that of an actual reader, all the names will be deemed invalid, and your having read them a pointless exercise.

Gerald La Gripe
Marshall Silverwind III
Barrington Riff
Henderson Cohn
Rip Schwantz

Deirdre Mazursky
Lou Ellen Wimpf
Truly Awful
Ronzo Snake
Threadna Woost

Melvin Rapture
Connington Willford
Diane Retreat
Tallullah Medulla
Kilbert Wax
Sonya Schnitz
Livia Blivel
Corporate Mess
Wickle Smith

Harraleigh Jumpkin
Blister Itkins
Softness La Rue
Temper Trenton
Giffersnail Rats
Cauley Foxm
Fwonz Rspteer
Lurington Whip
Ramanne Flake

IMPORTANT PSEUDONYMS

Actual Name	Pseudonym
Sander Batkin	Red Rouge
William Ferret	Harold Ferret
Simon Horowitz	Simon Twist
Leslie Maloney	The Green Tulip
Max Monk	Bart Crow
Dirk Flajeleski	Rock Flageleski
Peter Anturk	Crystal Ball
Lou Caavol	Priscilla Lirriam
Ordway Sussman	Pat Barron
Sol Kopintor	Lucian Racktillington, Jr.

IMPORTANT STAGE NAMES

Actual Name	Stage Name
Larry Snerd	Rock Crag
Dunce Wiener	Jack Wellington
Linda Pincewitz	Linda Love
Samuel Dorgin	Wong
Susan Tesslitz	Salonica Sizzle

IMPORTANT NICKNAMES

Actual Name	*Nickname*
Bill Steignitz	The Nitz
Marilyn Doosome	Dooz
Hildy Conklin	Miss Muffet
Jason La Pante	Old Cheese
Carrington Ramsey	The Whip
Paul Mosney	Sinker
Henry Wisstel	Lucky Hank
Jennifer Rasmusser	Goopy
Winston Hofritz	Nickle Nose

IMPORTANT FANTASY NAMES

Actual Name	*Fantasy Name*
Margie Dumster	Lorraine Bleedlove
Don Tiggle	Steel Tong
Benjamin Rappaport	Art Terrific
Comston Black	Panama Cool
George Washington Baily	Onyx
Martha Whipple	Luna

IMPORTANT ALIEN NAMES

Jzzzzzxv ljljljljlmmmxo	Landor Moonor
Juuuuiioououuou-ouuouououounx	#a*E?":%#
Tandor	Woooooooz Moooooooox
Poonitz	David Moooooooox
Weonkkkk	Reeeedle Deeeeedle

IMPORTANT INVISIBLE NAMES

Actual Name	*Invisible Name*
Ian Lester	
Barbara Annis	
Rosemary Fleur	
Diego Peersiflage	
Teddy Linhart	
Jared Gordon	
Milt Wolfson	
Chris Hunt	
Ed Brown	
Alan Pasternak	
Al Kilgore	
Alice Fixx	
LaMont Cranston	

IMPORTANT REPEATING NAMES
(ECHO NAMES)

Jack, Jack, Jack, jack

Peter, Peter, Peter, peter
Billy, Billy, Billy, billy
Max, Max, Max, max
Donald, Donald, Donald, donald
Sam, Sam, Sam, Sam, sam
Milly, Milly, Milly, milly
Sarah, Sarah, Sarah, sarah

Not every name can be a repeater. Notice how the following names do not repeat:

Blanche
Roderick
Joe
Carol
Bob
Wilster
Jason
Marsha
Corky
Belden

IMPORTANT END NAMES

Lewis Burke Frumkes

Horoscope

CAPRICORN—The Goat   Dec. 22–Jan. 20

There will be dark changes around you in the early weeks. Your marriage will be terminated. You will lose your job. A nuclear war will break out which may threaten your inner tranquillity. Avoid travel at this time, especially out of the house. Do not be discouraged, as Venus will be moving up and down your cusp between the fourteenth and twenty-second. Towards the end of the month things will improve. Radiation levels will have subsided, and new job opportunities await you. Pay close attention to the Emergency Broadcasting System.

AQUARIUS—The Water Bearer
Jan. 21–Feb. 18

Mammon enters your second house through the rear door. Money will appear seemingly out of nowhere. There will be opportunities for romance, some with the opposite sex. Take advantage of these opportunities. By the fifteenth, Mars will enter your new moon, and turbulence will follow. You will be arrested. The money which appeared from nowhere earlier in the month now proves to come from a local bank robbery. Mars will remain in your moon for five to ten years. Use this time to establish new friendships, particularly with the warden.

PISCES—THE FISHES   FEB. 19–MAR. 20

Your marriage, which was never very good anyway, will be in further jeopardy during the early part of the month, when your partner leaves you for the third baseman on the Milwaukee Brewers. You have an accident on the twelfth. It is of a minor sort involving your Toyota and a Boeing 747. After the twenty-fifth, your health takes a turn for the better, and you are once again able to cough. Now is a good time to complete old projects, finishing an orgasm begun during the Johnson administration, or painting the other half of the house. In any event, keep yourself busy, for next month you will turn into a large moth.

ARIES—THE RAM   MAR. 21–APR. 20

Seeds planted earlier in the year bear fruit at this time. Spray with Malathion to get rid of white flies and aphids, then fertilize. Avoid travel, especially to Easter Island. Mid-month your children will begin to get on your nerves. Spray with Malathion and send them to Easter Island. Get out of the way on the twentieth as Jupiter moves toward your rising Pluto. By the end of the month, your kids will return from Easter Island. Use this time to overdose on Seconal.

TAURUS—THE WINGED BULL
APR. 21–MAY 21

This is an excellent month to advance your career. If you are a Mafia lieutenant, try to cement a relationship with the "Boss of Bosses." Assuming you are successful, you will become the new "Boss of Bosses"; if not, there is no need to read next month's horoscope. For the time being avoid small restaurants, even if the soup du jour is cream of tomato. Make sure no one enters your home without proper identification. After Neptune sinks into Sicily sometime around the twenty-sixth, you may once again gargle with anisette.

GEMINI—THE TWINS   MAY 21–JUNE 21

Heed the advice of fortune cookies during the first three weeks of the month, paying special attention to stock tips. Travel. Plan a trip to Capistrano next August to see the psychiatrists, or Martha's Vineyard to see the swallows. Later in the month, with Mercury rising, blackouts will occur in your area. Avail yourself of excellent bargains on Madison and Fifth avenues. Take the opportunity to caulk windows.

CANCER—THE CRAB   JUNE 21–JULY 22

During the period from the first to the tenth, you will feel isolated from those you love. As Venus crosses paths with dilating Mercury, your health will suffer and you will discover that you are both schizophrenic and Napoleon Bonaparte.

Near the end of the month the schizophrenia will disappear, and you will wonder what to do with the two thousand prisoners captured during your New Jersey campaign. This is a good question. Perhaps you could put them to work mining anchovies in New Hampshire.

LEO—The Lion   July 23–Aug. 23

Now is the time to lose extra pounds gained during your stint as a prune dip for Barricini. Take off the old T-shirt with "Goodyear" stamped across the front and return it to Dr. Atkins. About this time a new romance begins. It is a narcissistic relationship, and you spend two glorious weeks chasing yourself around the room. As Saturn gives birth to a new moon, job possibilities surface. You accept an offer to become "first broom" for the Department of Sanitation.

VIRGO—The Virgin   Aug. 24–Sept. 23

Toward the fourteenth you will be the subject of much notoriety. It will be revealed that you are the illegitimate son of Howard Hughes and the Chase Manhattan Bank. Life becomes a blank check, and you are almost able to pay the rent on your studio apartment. At this time friends prove their loyalty to you by asking for interest-free loans. On the twenty-sixth you try a new cologne called "Beef" and are bitten by a large dog.

LIBRA—The Scales   Sept. 24–Oct. 23

As promised, this month looks to be a real winner. Venus, Mars, Pluto, and Jupiter are racing frantically alongside your full moon. You will become president of the United States, inherit $100 million, and fall deeply in love with a parrot named Gene, all before the fifteenth. After that it's dicey.

SCORPIO—The Scorpion   Oct. 24–Nov. 22

Due to Venus in Cancer, you should avoid marrying out of your income bracket until after the fifth. From the sixth to the sixteenth sudden emotional shifts will cause you to attack the international balance of payments through letters to *Newsweek* magazine. While this condition persists, it will be accompanied by soft music and winning gin hands. Avoid knocking throughout the period, unless you are under two.

SAGITTARIUS—The Archer
Nov. 23–Dec. 21

Because of an equilibrium of planetary influences this month, you will be possessed of full spiritual harmony. Use this to your advantage by founding a new religion, or taking naps. As Leo sits on Scorpio about the twentieth, clouds will form on your horizon, and you will die. Things will pick up around the twenty-eighth when you move to Queens and meet others of your persuasion. A hoary stranger will tell you that life is just a bowl of cherries. The hoary stranger is not playing with a full deck.

About The Author

Found between Fruit and Frustration in *The Reader's Guide to Periodical Literature,* Lewis Burke Frumkes is also a humorist whose work has delighted readers in the pages of *Punch, Travel & Leisure, Harper's,* and *The New York Times.*

Given his druthers, says Frumkes, or for that matter anyone else's druthers, he would rather spend his time on his ranch in Bajo De Playa, training anchovies.

Catalog

If you are interested in a list of fine Paperback
books, covering a wide range of subjects
and interests, send your name and address,
requesting your free catalog, to:

McGraw-Hill Paperbacks
1221 Avenue of Americas
New York, N.Y. 10020